A SECRET BOND

Something in Mark Craven's tone made Beth uneasy.

"Has it not occurred to you that your guardian takes that word 'guardian' rather literally? How many girls your age are guarded so they cannot escape?

"When are you going to break your bonds?"

MY DEAREST LOVE

EMILIE LORING

MY DEAREST LOVE

BANTAM BOOKS
TORONTO · NEW YORK · LONDON · SYDNEY

*This low-priced Bantam Book
has been completely reset in a type face
designed for easy reading, and was printed
from new plates. It contains the complete
text of the original hard-cover edition.*

MY DEAREST LOVE

*A Bantam Book / published by arrangement with
Little, Brown and Company, Inc.*

PRINTING HISTORY

Little, Brown edition published March 1954
2nd printing ...... April 1954
3rd printing ... November 1954
Grosset & Dunlap edition published September 1955
2nd printing ...... May 1956   3rd printing .. February 1957
4th printing .... January 1958

Bantam edition / May 1959

2nd printing .... March 1960	9th printing . September 1965
3rd printing ... January 1963	10th printing ... October 1966
4th printing ...... June 1964	11th printing ..... April 1967
5th printing ...... June 1964	12th printing .... March 1968
6th printing .... August 1964	13th printing ..... June 1968
7th printing .. November 1964	14th printing ... October 1968
8th printing ..... April 1965	15th printing .... August 1969
16th printing .... January 1970	

New Bantam edition / August 1971

2nd printing ...... June 1972	6th printing .... October 1974
3rd printing .... March 1973	7th printing .. November 1975
4th printing .... August 1973	8th printing ...... April 1977
5th printing .... August 1974	9th printing .... January 1981
10th printing .... January 1983	

Cover photo courtesy of Freelance Photographers Guild.

ISBN 0-553-22860-9

Published simultaneously in the United States and Canada

Bantam Books are published by Bantam Books, Inc. Its trademark, consisting of the words "Bantam Books" and the por-
trayal of a rooster, is Registered in U.S. Patent and Trademark
Office and in other countries. Marca Registrada. Bantam
Books, Inc., 666 Fifth Avenue, New York, New York 10103.

PRINTED IN THE UNITED STATES OF AMERICA

H   19 18 17 16 15 14 13 12 11 10

MY DEAREST LOVE

With startling unexpectedness the western sky crimsoned in streaks as though the sun, exasperated with the slow process of tinting, had flung his color brush straight at the horizon.

Beth Gilbert stood on the station platform, head tilted back on her slim throat while she watched the magnificent process, and drew a long, unsteady breath. Home, she thought. Home at last. Automatically she looked around for the Bradfords' motorcar but it was not in sight. How could she expect it to be there when she had let no one know she was coming?

For a moment she regretted the impulse that had led her to tear up the telegram announcing her arrival so that she could fling open the door and take them by surprise. But the anticipation of that moment brought a smile back to her lips and laughter to her eyes as she ran down the steps from the station platform to the sidewalk and waved her hand to the driver of the village's one and only taxi.

He slid out from under the wheel and held the door open for her.

"Where to, miss?"

"The Manor," she said. She laughed softly. "Don't you recognize me, Sam?"

The taxi driver looked at the lovely, animated face now flushed with excitement, at the waves of bronze hair that appeared under the small green hat.

"Miss Beth!" he exclaimed. "You've grown up such a lot I wouldn't have known you."

"Grown up! I'm nearly twenty-two," she said, so indignantly that the driver chuckled as he climbed back into his seat and started the car. "You sound like Chris—Mr. Bradford," the girl went on. "I've finished

boarding school and traveled through Europe and
had a season in New York and he still calls me a kid.
Don't people ever grow up to their families, Sam?"

In answer to her half-laughing, half-earnest question the driver replied, "Not to their mothers, at any
rate. Mine still worries for fear I'll forget my raincoat
and fusses over me when I have a cold. And I'll never
see fifty again."

"This time," the girl said rebelliously, "they've
simply got to realize I've grown up."

"I suppose," the driver said tactlessly, "it's different
when they aren't your real family," and devoted his
attention to driving.

But they are my family, Beth thought. Nan—Chris
—Ted—they were the only family she had. The fact
that they were not related, that Chris had taken over
the duty of being her guardian on the death of her
father, did not make them less her family. And the
Manor. Surely that was her home, the only home she
had, the only home she wanted. This homecoming,
in fact, she secretly hoped would be her last; that she
could stay forever without having to travel again, to
see the world, to have a social season in New York so
that she would not, in Chris's laughing words, become
too provincial.

Beth pulled off her hat and let the crisp autumn
air slide through the heavy masses of bronze hair like
caressing fingers. As the creaking taxi slowed for a
curve at the top of a hill she could see sweeping fields
divided with more or less regularity by stone walls,
not scraggly and unkempt, but well-laid, thrifty-look-
ing walls. The foliage was crimson and gold, making
a gorgeous frame for the bay, beyond which the sea
stretched out illimitably. The distant hills resembled
mammoth Persian rugs of the softest, most marvelous
coloring. A flock of crows in a distant cornfield which
had been stripped of its crop made the air vibrate
with their hoarse calls. Not far away a bronzed grackle
pecked at the ground, one yellow, beadlike eye fixed
on the girl.

Home, she thought again. She would be safe here.

Safe! Or perhaps the whole thing had been her imagination, that idea that she had been followed in Europe, the impression that her room had been searched repeatedly, her luggage ransacked, although nothing had been taken. At any rate, even if—for some unknown reason—she had been followed, the whole thing had stopped abruptly a month before. There was no reason to be afraid.

"Remember Julia!" she told herself. How many times she had said that in the past few months, trying to assure herself that everything was all right, that she was exaggerating. "Remember Julia!" And the phrase always brought back her guardian's face when he used the words, his tender mouth, his steady eyes, as he cautioned her to remember the wild exaggerations of Julia Seagreave, his uncle's young widow, which had become a family joke.

Beth peered eagerly out of the taxi window, watching for the first sight of the Manor, which had been her home for the past eight years, and represented her only family since her father's sudden and tragic death two years before. Even now she winced in pain as she thought of it, though Nan Bradford had taken to her heart as well as to her home the lonely child Beth had been.

The taxi was moving along a narrow road, the banks of which were starred with purple asters and the red leaves of the scrub oak. The trunk of a giant elm was aflame with scarlet ivy. And there at last was the Manor and home!

The sun transformed the western windows of the great brick house into sheets of flame as they approached it. It was a capacious, massive mansion which a Bradford of several generations back had built to please his southern wife. She had named it the Manor and the Manor it had remained ever since. Each succeeding owner had added to his holdings of land and to the house, till now it looked what it had been for a hundred years and more, a home. The atmosphere of the place suggested all sorts of family rites, the coming and passing of souls; the departure of youth and its homecomings; weddings; balsam-scented Christmases; the jubilant, exultant bells of holidays.

After the taxi had stopped, Beth Gilbert sat for a moment, blinking the tears out of her eyes. I wonder, she thought, if there is another house like this in all the world? Why, oh why, did Chris insist on sending me away to school and to Europe and packing me off to New York for the winter? Everything I want in life is here: graciousness, country living, Nan with her understanding, Ted with his fun, Chris—

Perhaps, after all, things would be different now. Ted was still recuperating from a long illness, unable to return to college, and carrying on his studies with the help of a tutor. Chris was going to marry Evelyn Furnas. His mother had written to Beth about the engagement, making the announcement with unusual restraint but adding a fervent prayer for her son's happiness, almost as though, Beth had thought at the time, she was unsure of it. And Chris's younger brother Ted had added a flippant postscript to his mother's letter: *The Duchess is going to marry Chris. I guess I'm spoiled, having you and Mother around the house. I like warm, real people.*

"Anyone would think you'd never seen the Manor before," the taxi driver chuckled.

Beth snapped out of her absorption, paid him, adding a tip and a smile which began in her eyes and warmed her vivid face before it touched her lips.

"Leave my luggage out here," she said in a conspiratorial whisper, "and coast down to the road before you start up the motor. I want to surprise them."

She opened the door and went inside on tiptoe. The doors leading from the wide hallway to the drawing room on the right and Chris's study on the left were both closed. Standing motionless in the hallway, her back turned to Beth, was a girl in maid's uniform. Something rigid in her posture indicated that she was deliberately eavesdropping.

From behind the door of the study came an unusual sound for the Manor, the sound of a woman's raised, angry voice. Beth stood rooted until the end of that bitter conversation.

"I mean it, Chris. Make your choice. Either you tell Beth Gilbert she doesn't live here any more or our engagement is at an end."

There was a sound of rapid footsteps inside the room and the maid ran noiselessly down the hall and out of sight. Then the door of the study was flung open as though blown by a high wind.

Evelyn Furnas stole a glance at her companion. He stood by an open window looking out on the garden, his dark hair roughened by the breeze; the sunset glow colored his face and deepened the gray of his eyes. She shrugged her shoulders. Where were his thoughts now, she wondered. Surely not upon her. Well, better to have the ordeal over as soon as possible.

Christopher Bradford heard the quick indrawn breath and turned to look inquiringly at her.

"What is it, Evelyn? Anything troubling you?"

"Nothing. Only—"

She flushed to her hair under her fair skin; her blue eyes hardened as they met the sympathetic gray ones of the man. With an impatient movement she brushed back an imaginary lock of her bright hair, too elaborately coifed ever to have a curl disarranged. Her lips, of the type which in age harbor fine, radiating lines, were tremulous for a moment, then steady as she continued.

"There *is* something. Chris, I have decided that our engagement is a mistake. I want to be freed from it." She had her courage well in hand now, her color was normal. She looked at him serenely from cold eyes.

His eyes reddened darkly, his gray eyes were black but his voice cool as he asked, "Why, Evelyn?"

"Why?" Her voice had a razor edge and the accumulated dissatisfaction of months was in the words she poured forth. "Why? Because when I marry a man I want him for myself. I don't intend to share him with relatives and every neighbor within a radius of twenty miles who has a fancied grievance. You and I never plan to go anywhere but what just at the last moment someone rushes in and demands, 'Where's Chris? I *must* see Chris.' Instead of asserting your rights and declaring that you can't be detained, you listen to all they have to say, regardless of the fact that I am waiting."

A smile illuminated the gravity of Bradford's face. "Oh, it isn't quite as bad as that, Evelyn. I admit that I am a sort of—of catch-all for confidences, but beware of the lure of exaggeration. Remember Julia! Is that the sum and substance of your dissatisfaction with me as a prospective husband?" He looked at her keenly.

She flushed with indignation at the lightness of his tone. Tiny blue flames flared in her eyes.

"No, it is not. You are mad about this dead and alive place and I loathe it."

Bradford's eyes glowed dangerously but he kept a grip of steel on his temper. He spoke quietly. "When my father died he made me sole executor of his estate. The property has grown until the agricultural part of it alone is a profession. The real estate comprises almost half the buildings in town. As to the tenants"— there was a twinkle in the gray eyes—"it takes about one man's time to give them advice. However, if you marry me you won't have to live here all the time. My income is sufficient to give you months in town, though it is true that my interests are here. I am not a city man. I love the open and I think I mean something in this community."

"Then you expect me to be stuck here all your life, even if you manufacture the Gilbert formula?"

"What do you know about the Gilbert formula?"

Chris's face was suddenly grim, set, the face of a stranger. His eyes bored into hers. Her face crimsoned under his glance until it seemed as though the blood must ooze through the fair skin.

"Why—why," she stammered. She moistened her dry lips with the tip of her tongue. "Only what everyone else knows. That Mr. Gilbert left some new formula with you and fell unconscious in your driveway that very night and died. The police thought he had been deliberately knocked down and robbed. His pockets were empty. Some people even said—murder. And his laboratory assistant disappeared at the same time. Lately I've heard talk that you are going to manufacture the formula yourself."

"Who talked?"

"I don't remember," she said evasively.

"Sure of that?"

"Of course I'm sure," she flared. "I don't know anything about the old formula and I don't care. But there's one thing I do care about. Maybe Mr. Gilbert didn't leave you his formula but he did leave you his daughter. At least, he left her to your father—"

"My father promised Gilbert that Beth could make her home at the Manor until she married."

"But you didn't promise," Evelyn reminded him.

"When my father left me his estate, he expected me to assume his other responsibilities. Besides, I am Beth's guardian."

"But you were only twenty-two, Chris, when your father died. You shouldn't be saddled with the girl. She's nothing to you." Evelyn added more sharply, "Or is she?"

"I'm ashamed of you, Evelyn. She's only a kid."

Evelyn's eyes fell on a shabby, cheap frame on his desk, holding a photograph of a lean, lanky, very young girl, her arms filled with puppies. The photograph had obviously been tinted by a young and unpracticed hand, for the girl's hair was a commercially convincing oleomargarine yellow, her cheeks and lips a startlingly lurid red, her frock a brilliant blue, the vividness of which was slightly ameliorated by the greenish-brown puppies she held in her arms.

"What a freak," Evelyn laughed. "Why on earth do you keep that eyesore in this charming room? It's the only jarring note."

"It doesn't jar me," Chris said. "Because, you see, I remember a shy, long-legged youngster on her first Christmas in a strange home, who colored the picture herself and fairly burst with pride when she gave it to me. But, Evelyn, there's one thing I must know."

She broke in quickly as though to forestall his question. "There is one thing *I* want to know. Do you intend to keep her here?"

"No persuasion of yours could make me hurt her or ignore my promise to her father."

"Or take chances on losing the control of that formula," Evelyn snapped.

"Evelyn!"

"You needn't bite my head off. Do you choose her instead of me?"

"If you want to put it that way," Chris replied steadily. "I would prefer to say that the choice is between my honor and you."

"I mean it, Chris. Make your choice. Either you tell Beth Gilbert she doesn't live here any more or our engagement is at an end."

She crossed the room quickly and flung open the door of the study as though it were blown by a high wind.

For a long moment they looked at one another with startled eyes: the blond girl with burning blue eyes, the bronze girl with wide, shocked brown eyes. Then Evelyn observed the other more closely, the lovely oval of her face made vivid by the constantly changing expression, like waters rippled by a breeze, the beautifully fitting simple suit and the small green hat that brought out russet tints in her hair.

"What are you doing here?" she asked insolently.

It was Chris who answered. "She has every right to be here. This is her home. Evelyn, I want you to know my ward, Elizabeth Gilbert."

II

"This is your ward?" Evelyn's incredulous tone sent a wave of color over Beth's face. Then she remembered her father's words: "A rude comment is an indictment of the person who makes it, not of the person to whom it is made."

She lifted her chin and faced the hostile girl, her eyes level, an unconscious dignity in her manner.

"Beth! Welcome home, child," Chris said. His arm went around her and he gave her a brotherly kiss on the cheek.

"Beth!" A very tall, thin boy hailed her from the top of the stairs and came clattering down. He swung her off her feet exuberantly and then, grinning, set her on her feet. "Jeepers! Why didn't you let us know you were coming? I'd have met you. I've got a new car I want to show you anyhow. Am I glad to see you! Now we can have some swell—" He broke off to ask, "How long have you been here?"

Beth's faint flush as she answered, "I just this moment arrived," was observed by Evelyn, whose eyes narrowed thoughtfully.

"Then Mother doesn't know you're back?"

"Not yet."

"She'll be in the drawing room. It's about time for tea. That's why—"

"Why you were galloping down those stairs," Beth said with a gurgle of laughter. She looked up at his clear, handsome face, at the gray eyes so like Chris's, at the finely modeled lips beginning to show evidence of the strength and decision of maturity.

Ted winked at her and then added, with a courtliness which no amount of boyish roughness could conceal, "Aren't you going to join us for tea, Evelyn?"

"Thank you, no." The pink showed under her skin again. "I must go home."

"I'll see you to your car." Chris followed her down the hallway as she walked swiftly away, without a second glance or a word to Beth. When the outside door had closed behind them, the boy gave a long whistle.

"Does it strike you that the Duchess is constantly in a state of bad temper?" he inquired. "It beats me how old Chris stands it. She is too perfect for me. I think you are a darned sight prettier."

"Thank you, sir," Beth said with an effort to be gay.

"When I marry," the boy went on in the tone of one who lays down the law, "it will be to a girl who will let me rumple her hair if I want to. But Evelyn always looks as though she had just walked out of a beauty parlor and heaven help anyone who musses up a single curl."

"When you marry! Hear the infant talk," Beth mocked, and this time the gaiety in her voice was unforced and genuine. "If the little Blossom could only hear him!"

Ted colored at her reference to the girl who was the current object of a schoolboy crush and about whom he had written her during the summer.

"Infant, indeed! Who's talking to whom? Just wait until Chris starts calling us the kids. You'll see. Though I must say you look like a knockout. It shook Evelyn's confidence to find she isn't the prettiest woman around here any more. She didn't like it a little bit."

"She didn't like *me* a little bit," Beth said soberly.

"I'd hate to have her say that to me," Ted growled.

"My faithful watchdog!" Beth laughed.

"Don't forget you are talking to a college man," he boasted. His eyes shadowed as he continued impatiently, "Only I'm not. Those doctors are making me wait another half year before I go back. And I could have been on the baseball team next season."

The boy's eyes held a suspicious brightness which

brought a lump to the girl's throat. She patted his arm.

"Never mind. Nan wrote that you've already gained pounds and pounds, and this tutor of yours is keeping you up with your classes. By the time the baseball season starts you'll be raring to go."

"Do you really mean it? Beth, it's swell having you home. A real sister couldn't be nicer. And it's true about the studies. Smithy's a fine tutor, though a bit more of a slave driver than I could wish. It was lucky for me when he answered Chris's ad, though it stumps me why a man of his brains should be willing to settle down in a country place like this instead of teaching in a university. Hey, I'm starving. Come have tea, Slim, and see Mother."

"Just a kid." Chris's words echoed in Beth's mind. Why did she resent them so much now when she never had minded in the past?

"Don't call me Slim any more," she said, so sharply that the boy was taken aback. "When I was a lanky, thin-necked child, with abnormally long legs, who looked as though she might have nibbled one side of Alice's mushroom in Wonderland, it was all right. But I've *grown up*."

"You are getting as touchy as the Duchess," Ted said in disgust. "And that girl had better go slow. Chris is no fool. He may seem easy but he won't stand any funny business with a girl. More likely to go caveman and take a club to her."

"Ted!"

He nodded his head. "You'll remember what I say if you ever try to get engaged to someone he doesn't approve of. He can be all Scotch granite. I ought to know. I've tried to chip it. So watch your step, Slim— Beth, I mean. You are so impulsive I'm always afraid you'll do some reckless thing when Chris and I aren't around to pull you out of it."

"I wouldn't dare move without your approval," she gibed.

"Then move to the drawing room, will you, before I starve?"

"I'll go up to my room first. I feel so messy after my trip."

"You look like someone's dreamboat but if you want to make improvements on perfection, I suppose you must. Only hurry," he urged her.

"Five minutes," Beth promised.

But ten minutes later she was still standing in the middle of her familiar bedroom, which Mrs. Bradford had decorated for her years before, with its pale yellow walls and soft blue rug and casement windows opening on tall trees riotous with color. She stood quite still, her hands clenched at her sides.

Chris's engagement had been broken because of me, she repeated over and over dully to herself. Because of me. He has done more for me than anyone in the world, given me a home and security and happiness. And I've hurt him like that.

Why, she wondered, had Evelyn Furnas hated her so, even before seeing her? They had never met before. But, that, troubling as it was, mattered less than Chris's unhappiness. What could she do about it? She forced her mind back to her problem. . . . I'll have to go away and get a job. The allowance Chris gives me for clothes and fun isn't enough to live on and perhaps I haven't a right to that. I've never asked what my father left for him. I just took it for granted.

She tossed off her hat and ran her fingers through the soft masses of her hair. But what kind of job can I get that will support me? Typing? I learned that at school but it is rusty now. Chris promised I'd have a home here until I marry.

Marriage! That would be another way of freeing Chris from the burden she had become. But to whom? There had been proposals enough in the past two years but no one whom she had seriously considered marrying. No one who had even touched the surface of her heart. And that was not good enough.

"How will I know," she had asked her father once as a very small girl, when he had finished reading a "happy ever after" fairy tale, "when to get married so I can be happy ever after?"

He had not laughed at her, but considered her question gravely. "You'll know," he told her, "when you love someone deep in your heart, not just a little, but completely. You'll know when your idea of happiness is not being *made* happy but making someone else happy." When she had looked perplexed he had said, "Don't worry about it now. You will understand when the time comes."

Beth caught sight of herself in the mirror, the drooping mouth and unhappy face. And an hour ago I thought I was coming home to safety and peace. Why, when the world is so beautiful, must life be so disappointing? There is no place on earth where I really belong. I have no claim to Chris's loyalty and his—his kindness. After breaking up his engagement I have not even the right to trouble him about my problems. I can't tell him how I was shadowed in Europe. It would sound as though I were appealing to his sympathy, making him feel that I was helpless, that I needed him. Depended on him.

She straightened her shoulders and met steadily the eyes of the girl in the mirror. "I'm ashamed of you, Beth! Stop being sorry for yourself. The Bradfords have given you eight wonderful years. It's your turn now. You can help Chris win back the girl he wants to marry."

She considered her expression critically, "And smile!" she ordered. A tremulous smile quivered on her lips and then broadened. "That's better."

She nodded to her reflection and then, waving her hand to the girl in the mirror, she left the room and ran down the stairs.

This time the door of the drawing room was open and she paused for a moment on the lowest step, looking in. Her throat tightened. Wherever she might have to go, this would always be home. This lived-in room, which was as welcoming as open arms.

It was a large room with a huge fireplace across one end in which a cheery fire of logs blazed and sizzled socially and confidentially as the flames wriggled and flared up the chimney. At right angles to it stood a capacious davenport. On the opposite side of the room French doors opened onto a terrace that, in summer, was gay with beach chairs and umbrellas, and musical with the twitter of birds.

An old-fashioned tea wagon had been wheeled into the room. An antique hot-water kettle sent forth a friendly, purring jet of steam; a gay cozy shrouded the teapot. Toast and scones were on a muffin stand. Before the wagon sat a woman of perhaps forty-nine, though she looked younger. Her dark hair, gently touched with white at the temples, was parted on one side and waved close to her ears, from which hung Oriental-looking hoops of gold. Her unlined face had the color and freshness of perfect health. Her heavily lashed gray eyes were soft and glowing. She was slender, with only a suggestion of the roundness of maturity. Her lips alone showed age; there was a slight tension about them when her face was in repose that evidenced she had lived and suffered.

She looked up with a smile which made her charming face radiant.

"Beth! My dear child. Welcome home!" She held out both hands and Beth ran over to take them in her own and, bending over, gave the older woman a swift little kiss.

"It's good to be here," she said huskily.

"We've missed you. There's a quality of gaiety about you that is like sunshine in the house. Ted is practically leaping with delight. By the way," she added anxiously, "how do you think he looks?"

"Much, much better than I expected. I told him he'd be back in college and playing baseball by spring."

"I know. He was tremendously bucked up about it. You do us all good."

"Not Chris." Beth's voice broke. "Not Chris. Oh, Nan, I've done Chris so much harm."

Mrs. Bradford looked at the girl quickly and then at the tea she was pouring. "Cream or lemon, Beth?" she asked as absorbedly as though the fate of nations hung on the girl's reply.

"Cream."

The girl stared unseeingly at the capable hands with their exquisite rings as she asked hesitatingly, "Has Chris been very happy in his engagement?"

A little flush tinged the older woman's face. "I gather you have met Evelyn."

"Yes, I—yes, she—"

"I suppose," Mrs. Bradford said slowly, "every woman sees her children through rosy glasses. But Chris—he is so big and vital and unselfish, and Evelyn Furnas is—well, small and bloodless and grasping. Sometime you may know what it means to a mother to see her boy, the very light of her eyes, make a wrong choice. Mind you, I may be wrong. I keep reminding myself that I am not marrying Evelyn, that I shall not have to live with her and see her grow more self-centered and cold, year by year. But it's terribly hard, because Chris is—well, he's just Chris," with a shaky little laugh. "I'd give my life any time for my boys and yet I can do nothing to help if they make unhappy marriages. They have been brought up with traditions; there has never been a divorce or separation in the family. And yet I feel that Chris is steering straight for the rocks."

"But if you are right about her, Nan, how did Chris—"

"She deliberately snared him. I felt so from the beginning."

"I suppose that most girls try to make the man they love, love them, don't they?" Beth admitted honestly.

"They don't use Evelyn's tactics. I never believed she loved him. But her father lost most of his money a year ago and Chris, after all, is the leading man in this part of the country. But lately—" Her voice trailed off uncertainly.

"Lately?" Beth prompted her.

"All summer her parents had a house guest, a man named Mark Craven. He is rumored to be a man of immense wealth and sometimes I've hoped—and he's staying on at the inn this fall. Well, anyhow," she added incoherently, "I keep telling myself, Chris isn't married yet! He isn't married yet!"

"Then," Beth said breathlessly, "if the engagement were broken, you wouldn't mind?"

"I'd be a very happy woman."

"Nan." For a moment Beth hesitated, and then the story of the conversation she had overheard came tumbling out. The only thing she forgot was her sight of the strange parlormaid listening at the door of the study.

"Thank heaven!" Nan Bradford said fervently.

"But will Chris be terribly unhappy? Have I—" Beth blinked away her tears—"have I been to blame?"

"You!" The older woman smiled brilliantly. "I have always hoped that someday Chris would discover that you have grown up."

The color flooded Beth's cheeks and ebbed away again. "He hasn't," she confessed ruefully. "But it's about time."

"What's about time?" asked Christopher Bradford from the doorway.

His mother gave a swift look at his fine, clear-cut face, at his gray eyes, his dark hair, then she busied herself about the tea-things.

"Will you have cream as usual, Chris?"

"Thank you, yes. About time for what, Mother?"

"I thought," his mother said, "you were bringing Evelyn to tea."

"She won't be here. In fact, she broke our engagement this afternoon."

"My dear, I hope—"

He smiled tenderly at his mother. "It's a shock," he admitted, "but there's no lasting damage. Nothing for you to grieve about. A mutual mistake, that was all. For some time we have both been realizing that we had taken a transitory feeling for an enduring one."

"And everything's all right now?"

"Everything is all right," he assured her.

From the doorway a brisk voice said, "Don't try to keep me out. Where's Chris? Something is wrong."

III

The parlormaid appeared at Anne Bradford's side, pink spots in her cheeks, her eyes angry. She was a pretty girl whom Beth had never seen before. Or rather, whom she had seen once before, listening outside the door of Christopher Bradford's study.

"She insists on seeing Mr. Christopher," she explained. "I can't keep her out."

Mrs. Bradford smiled. "It's quite all right, Rose. Mrs. Mumford lived in this family for years and she is always welcome here."

The maid stepped back without another word and allowed a small, wiry, elderly woman to enter.

"There you are, Chris," the newcomer said, with the familiarity of an old nurse to whom her charges never grow up, as soon as she had controlled her indignation sufficiently to produce a voice from her wrinkled, parchmentlike throat. "Miss Anne, that new maid of yours with her pretty doll face and no chin—I know the type, weak, weak as water—tried to keep me out. Beth!" She forget her anger as she beamed at the girl. "This is a surprise. My, how you've grown up!"

"Mummy!" Beth squealed in delight, calling the old woman by the name with which the Bradford children had endowed her during the years when she was their nurse. "What beautiful words! You are the only one who appreciates me."

The shrewd eyes studied her fondly. "Hmm, I doubt that. I guess a lot more people than Mummy have discovered that you've turned into a downright beauty. Now don't let it go to your head and spoil you," she added sharply. "I must say, no one would have guessed you'd blossom out so, when I think what a skinny child you were, all legs and eyes. I guess at that you won't be spoiled. Got too much sense and that same gaiety shining out of your eyes. As pretty as the girls in the movies, only—warmer, more real."

"Still a movie fan!" Beth teased her.

"What's wrong, Mummy?" Chris asked. "Anything I can do?"

"I want to talk to you. There's something on my mind you ought to know about. Something wrong going on. I'd have got here sooner only I ran into Mrs. Seagreave and Miss Furnas outside, quarreling like anything."

"Julia and Evelyn?" Mrs. Bradford said in surprise.

Martha Mumford nodded grimly. "And I heard Miss Furnas say she had broken her engagement. Chris, I—"

He patted her shoulder. "Don't be sorry for me, Mummy."

"Sorry!" the old woman exploded. "I'm tickled pink."

Mrs. Bradford concealed a smile behind her handkerchief.

"You never really knew Evelyn," Chris said tactfully.

"All I wanted to!" declared the irrepressible nurse. "Stuck-up thing. And now I guess she'll try to get that rich Craven man who's been hanging around here."

"Mummy." Mrs. Bradford's voice held a warning. She did not encourage gossip.

"Well, all I can say," the old woman declared stubbornly, "is that Mrs. Seagrave thinks the same thing. Told Miss Furnas to her face that she was after him. And your ex-fiancée"—with a glance at Chris—"said, considering the way Mrs. Seagreave had been asking him to her parties and all, she was no one to talk."

Chris endeavored to stop the conversation by going toward the door. "I'll be in the study when you want me," he said and went out of the room.

Martha Mumford looked after him with troubled eyes. "Just the same," she said to Mrs. Bradford, "the Lord be praised! Chris is free again. There's only one person in the world who was made for him. Sometime he'll wake up to it and then you'll see some courting. When he's really in love, he'll sweep a girl off her feet and straight into his arms, see if he don't. That Furnas girl was no homemaker. She's restless; she'd always have to be on the move." She turned to Beth. "You've been on the move a lot yourself, the last couple of years anyhow."

"Because Chris made me. I hate the life. Of course, I enjoy theaters, operas, pictures, and I adore the shops, but I don't have to live in the city to get all that. There is so much more to do in the country, always something or somebody who is being vitally interesting every minute."

"So you want to stay here now?" The old woman's eyes brightened.

Want to? Beth thought. That's my idea of heaven. And then she remembered Evelyn's angry voice saying, "Maybe Mr. Gilbert didn't leave you his formula but he did leave you his daughter. At least he left her to your father—" and Chris replying, "When my father left me his estate, he expected me to assume his other responsibilities." A responsibility, that was what she was. Just a kid. A burden. The words stung.

"For a visit," she said brightly. "Then I want to get a job."

"A job!" Both Martha Mumford and Mrs. Bradford looked at her in surprise.

Beth nodded. She forced her voice to sound enthusiastic. "I do love the country but I want to make a place for myself to have something that's my own."

"But—" The expression on Anne Bradford's face, the almost imperceptible shake of her head, checked the impetuous old woman. "Well," she grumbled, "I guess the young have to work things out for themselves."

"Hello, Mummy!" Ted came storming into the room and gave his old nurse a hug.

She smiled up at the tall boy who had been in her care from the time he was born until he outgrew the need of a nurse. "Getting a little fatter, aren't you, darling?"

"Gained four pounds the last month, Mummy," he assured her. "I'll bet you've come to consult Chris. Everyone does. Why don't you consult me? I'm twice the man he is," he added, with a laugh and a squaring of his thin shoulders.

She laughed back at him. "You're a handsome young one and you'll make the girls dance to your tune later, but just now it's brains and steadiness I'm after." She chuckled at his indignant expression. "After all, you can't expect to have the brains and maturity of a man ten years older. Heaven forbid. And look what happens to Chris. Every good-for-nothing—including me—comes traipsing here after him. It beats me why he doesn't run away."

There was a hint of perfume, a tapping of high heels, and Julia Seagreave, the young widow of Anne Bradford's brother, swept into the room. She was a tall, willowy woman with obtrusively blue eyes and rather prominent teeth, followed by a man of middle height with reddish hair beginning to thin at the temples, close-tipped mustache and greenish eyes which peered near-sightedly through thick horn-rimmed spectacles.

"Anne!" she gushed. "Do give me some tea. I'm almost *dead!* That wretched car of mine simply *fell to pieces* in front of your door. If Mr. Smith had not come so gallantly to my rescue I should have gone *utterly mad.* Beth! Evelyn just told me you were back." She turned away from Beth to her sister-in-law. "By the way, she told me she and Chris—"

"Beth, my dear," Mrs. Bradford interrupted her hastily, "this is Mr. Smith who has been of such help to Ted."

"I've heard grand things about you, Mr. Smith," Beth told him as she offered her hand.

The tutor displayed his own hands in warning.

"Nan, look!" Beth exclaimed in horror as she inspected the tutor's outstretched hands.

Anne Bradford shook her head reprovingly. "You

fell a victim to the lure of some pretty red leaves," she hazarded.

Smith colored. His smile gave charm to his rather mask-like face.

"One might suppose that a man of my age would know poison ivy when he saw it, mightn't one? I don't mind the discomfort, though my hands are so stiff I'm afraid I can't cope with a cup of tea, but my stupidity rankles. Besides, I have some correspondence to finish and I doubt whether I can thump it out on the typewriter."

"Let me help," Beth offered impulsively. "I've just been talking about getting a job and I really need to brush up on my typing." As the tutor hesitated she added persuasively, "It would be a great favor to me."

Anne Bradford watched her. How lovely Beth had become, though she seemed quite unconscious of it. And how unchanged in other ways. The same loyalty and charm, the same generosity that always attempted to disguise itself, to appear to be the receiver and not the giver.

"Thank you very much, Miss Gilbert," the tutor said. "Have you time to type a letter before dinner so I may get it off in the evening mail?"

"Certainly. Come back here in half an hour."

"Thank you again."

When he had left the room and gone upstairs, Julia said sharply, "Really, Beth, can't you be satisfied with Chris—oh, Evelyn told me she broke her engagement on your account. And now you are after the tutor."

"Julia!" Ted began furiously. "That's not true. Beth had nothing to do with it. And, in my opinion, old Chris is in luck!" In his exuberant relief he helped himself liberally from the muffin stand and, with a sigh of satisfaction, settled down beside his mother. "Cinnamon toast, too. Mmm!"

"Cream and two lumps, please," Julia demanded. "I'm just about *worn out*. And after I've consulted with Chris I must simply *race* home and dress for dinner. Mr. Craven is dining with me tonight. What I'll do after Chris goes away, I can't imagine. I'll be *lost* without his advice. Simply *demented.*"

"But Chris isn't planning to leave home," Mrs. Bradford exclaimed.

"Oh, I thought when he began to manufacture the Gilbert formula—"

"I don't know where you got that idea, Julia."

"*Everybody*, but *everybody* is talking about it. The formula that will simply *revolutionize* plastics, scrap everything we have—"

Seeing his mother's uneasiness, Ted leaped tactfully into the breach. "I say, that's a stunning hat, Julia. It makes you look about twenty. Wait until your tame millionaire sees you in that."

"You mean Mr. Craven?" the widow asked coquettishly. "I have been seeing him rather often. He's a most unusual man. Terribly fascinating. Such devastating charm and a sense of power that thrills me. Or frightens me. It's such a pleasure to meet a man with really sophisticated tastes. I believe Evelyn, the silly child, thinks he is interested in her."

Ted chuckled. "I wouldn't give much for Evelyn's chances if Craven gets a look at Beth."

"At Beth! Of all the absurd—"

"Ted!" Anne Bradford looked at Beth's flushed face and spoke quietly. "You know how I dislike personalities."

Julia got swiftly to her feet. "Well, if Mumford is going to keep Chris *forever*, I might as well rush. Ted, dear, start my car, will you? Tell Chris I simply must see him without delay."

When she had gone, Anne Bradford turned to speak to Beth, but the girl had slipped quietly out of the room and gone upstairs. Mrs. Bradford stood looking down at the dismantled tea wagon, a troubled look on her charming face. Surely Beth knew what Julia was like. She was too sensible to be hurt by her ugly accusations. No one who knew the girl would believe her capable of trying to ensnare men. But it was an unfortunate homecoming, with both Evelyn and Julia treating her as an alien, and not as what she was, the dearly beloved daughter of the house.

In the study, Chris pulled out a chair for his old nurse and smiled at her encouragingly.

"What's wrong, Mummy? It must be something very important to drag you away from your shop at this hour when all the girls are coming home from work. Who will be there to advise them about their hats and their beaux?"

She looked up at him with shrewd tenderness.

"The girls and their beaux can wait. I have something to tell you, but first—you may think me a meddling old fool, Chris. I'm glad the break has come between you and the Furnas girl. I've—I've prayed for it."

"I'm glad your mind is at ease about me. Now"— changing the subject with gentle finality—"what is the trouble? A leaky roof? Boys robbing your orchard?"

Martha Mumford shook her white head. Her lips settled into a grim line.

"It's deviltry all right, Chris, I expect, but not that kind. The trouble is—I don't know what kind it is. But something is going on, something I can feel but can't get hold of."

"You've been seeing too many movies," he accused her.

She shook her head and something in her gravity made him drop his teasing manner.

"I can't put my finger on it. Rumors, people doing queer things, but it adds up to something bad."

"Bad for whom?"

"For you, Chris," she said bluntly.

"Suppose you tell me about it," he said quietly.

"That's just it! I don't know what to tell. All I know is that since the announcement came a month ago that you were going to manufacture the Gilbert formula, something has been wrong. People are saying things—" She broke off abruptly.

"What things?"

"I don't know what's got into people!" she burst

out. "You're the pillar of this community. A month ago everyone said so. But now—I've heard people in the waffle shop talking and in the post office. About that formula. About how you got it. As though—as though," she went on and with an effort, "it was something you'd got hold of in an underhand way. Chris, someone is deliberately stirring up trouble for you."

She looked up and to her astonishment saw that he was not disturbed; instead, he was alert, interested, pleased. Actually pleased!

For a moment he sat absorbed in thought and then he made up his mind. "I'd like to tell you about it, Mummy. It helps to talk to someone, helps to clarify my own thinking. I don't want to worry Mother and Ted is too young."

"Go ahead," Martha told him. She folded her hands in her lap and looked steadily at him, knowing that when men waxed confidential they wanted a woman's whole attention.

"I'll have to go back a bit," he warned her. "Eight years, to be exact. Gilbert was an old friend of my father's. After his wife died he came to see my father, bringing Beth with him. He said he was devoting all his time to some laboratory experiments and he was afraid his daughter was being neglected. On the strength of his old friendship with Father, Gilbert asked him to let the child live here; in fact, to become her guardian. You know how Mother is— you were here at the time. She took Beth to her heart with a cordial friendliness and sympathy that made the child's thin little face luminous with happiness.

"I was at home at the time and Father called me in. He said that he had no right to make a promise that might not be fulfilled in case of his own death. Sometimes I wonder if he had a sort of presentiment that he had only a short time to live. Would I, he asked, carry on? Gilbert asked me to promise that Beth should live at the Manor until she married, which must be only with the approval of her guardian. Of course, I promised. I was a senior in college at the time and I remember that all he was asking me to do seemed a remote possibility, for Father would be here for years to take the responsibility, even if anything should happen to Beth's father.

"Well, as you know, Father died a few months after Beth made her home here. Two years ago, Gilbert came over in great excitement. Lord, that was an awful day! His work had been completed, he said, and he told me about the formula. It would provide a new kind of plastics that would have a tremendous impact on industry, making some fabrics obsolete, creating many that have been heretofore undreamed of. He was going to New York to discuss the matter with a man who was to become his partner.

"It seemed to me highly dangerous to carry the formula with him and I said so. Gilbert was amused. He said only three people knew about it: the man he was going to see in New York; his assistant, Larry Sergent; and myself. Anyhow, what he had with him wouldn't be of much use to anyone else.

"What did he mean by that?" Mumford asked.

"I don't know," Chris admitted. "I've been asking myself that question for twenty-four months, night and day. Well"—he drew a long breath—"you know what happened that night two years ago. Gilbert left us go to the train; he insisted on walking because he was overwrought and excited and thought the exercise would help him to relax and sleep. On the driveway he fell unconscious, or he was knocked down and robbed. Anyhow, when we found him his pockets were empty, the formula was gone, and Gilbert never spoke again."

"You must be worked up, Chris," Martha said anxiously. "I've never seen you nervous before."

"I know," he admitted. "I have a ridiculous impression every now and then that someone is listening. And that's impossible. There's no one in this house capable of eavesdropping and yet—"

"I've got something to say about that later on," Martha Mumford said. "Go on. This is as exciting as the movie I saw last night. *The Missing Heir*, it was called."

"Well," Chris said, "you know no suspicion would have been aroused about Gilbert's death if his assistant, Larry Sergent, had not disappeared that very same night. There was a lot of speculation then about Gilbert's empty pockets and the work he had been doing in such secrecy.

"Ever since his death I have had agents at work to trace Sergent but he disappeared as completely as though the earth had swallowed him. A month ago, I determined to smoke him out. So I informed the papers that the formula had been entrusted to me and I intended to put the product on the market. If I am a judge of human nature, Sergent will move heaven and earth to get my copy of the formula. If all Gilbert claimed is true, there are millions in it."

"What became of the man who was to be Mr. Gilbert's partner?"

"I have no idea, Mummy," Chris confessed. "Sometimes I wonder—Gilbert was so overwrought from work—whether the whole thing was a figment of his imagination. All I could find among his papers in regard to the alleged transaction and the partnership was a lot of unsigned memoranda and no names of any kind."

There was silence in the room for a while. Then Martha Mumford said thoughtfully, "Millions in it. And people are beginning to talk about you."

"That interests me. You see, Mummy, it looks as though someone is eager to discredit me before making claims of his own."

"But, Chris, there were rumors—people said Mr. Gilbert was knocked on the head."

Chris's lips set tightly. "He was."

"Then won't this mean danger for you?"

He smiled reassuringly down at the anxious old face. "Complications, adventure, thrills, perhaps. But not real danger. I have a suspicion the fight has started already."

"But suppose," she persisted, "Larry Sergent—killed Mr. Gilbert for the formula? Suppose he comes back? Did you ever see him?"

Chris shook his head.

"A photograph? A description?" Martha insisted.

Again the answer was negative.

"Then," Martha said, "he might be anyone."

Chris laughed outright and the sternness in his face melted away, leaving it young and eager. "Mummy! Think for a moment. We are in the country. The summer visitors have gone. A stranger would be unable to hide—he would be as conspicuous as a sore thumb."

"But there are people we don't really know anything about," she told him.

He grinned at her. "Name one," he said challengingly.

"I can name three without even thinking," she retorted. "Stone, the new butler at Colonel Haswell's; Mr. Mark Craven, who has been visiting the Furnas family and now is staying on all alone at the inn, though the season is over; and Mr. Smith, Ted's tutor."

Chris laughed outright. "What a collection," he chuckled. "A first-rate servant, a prominent millionaire, and an ex-college professor."

"But do you know positively," Martha asked, her eyes shrewd, "that any of them are what they claim to be? Could you prove it if you had to?"

He looked at her in surprise. "Why, I—"

"Because someone is acting mighty queer, Chris. There's a man meeting that new maid of yours. I noticed them the first time by accident because they met in the orchard back of my cottage where it's kind of retired. I saw the man lounging against a tree, his hat pulled down over his eyes. The girl came creeping through the trees and he struck a match three times like a signal.

"It was a queer way to do things. So I kept my eyes open. They met again last night. Same man. Same signal."

Chris laughed. "Those movies!"

Martha's sober face did not lighten. "Laugh if you want to, only I could feel something wrong. If he's got a clear conscience, why hide his face? If he's not doing something he's afraid to have found out, why meet Rose in that furtive way instead of coming out in the open to see her? In any case, you'd better keep an eye on that girl."

"Enter the stranger in disguise," Chris teased her.

"Maybe. I only hope it isn't—enter the murderer."

IV

The girl, slim and graceful in the long, pale yellow dinner dress, looked doubtfully at the girl in the mirror. What was wrong with her, she thought, that Evelyn Furnas had refused to marry Chris rather than have her in the house, that Julia Seagreave had accused her of wanting to break up Chris's marriage—fantastic thought!—and of flirting with Ted's tutor.

She selected a handkerchief, started for the door, and then returned, undecided, before her fingers had touched the knob.

I can't go on like this, she thought—not understanding what is wrong. I'll have to talk to Chris. Ever since I was fourteen I've talked things over with him. I'll ask him about Evelyn, see whether I can't undo the harm I've done. Only—Here her mind wandered from the immediate problem. Only, she thought, Chris did not seem to be heartbroken about Evelyn, and his mother, Ted and Martha Mumford had been frankly relieved that the engagement was at an end.

Beth moved restlessly to the open casement windows and stared unseeingly into the gathering darkness. I must tell Chris about being followed in Europe, she thought.

Curiously enough, it seemed less easy than it had been in the past to talk to Chris. Just a kid, he had said, and the words still rankled. She wasn't a kid. If she were to tell him about her experiences he would believe them the work of a child's vivid imagination, like Mummy, who was always trying to find parallels in daily life for the movies which were her constant delight.

No, she would not tell Chris. She would grapple

with her problem alone. Everyone within a radius of forty miles who had an ache or a pain, a debt or a dun, a marriage or a divorce, a refractory child or an irreverent grandchild, sooner or later came to consult Chris and drop their burdens of doubt and care on his shoulders. Ever since his father's death he had been the master of the house, and oh, how well he had carried the responsibility. It would have made insufferable prigs or careworn old men of most boys, but Chris had retained his genial happy nature, his power of clear constructive thinking, and his unfailing store of sympathetic understanding.

Beth waved to the shadowy girl in the mirror and went out into the hall. At the foot of the stairs, much too close to the closed doors of the study, Rose was standing again. Her cheeks had lost the color which had tinged them earlier in the afternoon. They were pale and her eyes held a furtive expression. As Beth watched her, the maid's hand stole out and touched the knob. Before she could turn it, Beth said crisply, "Mr. Bradford does not like to be disturbed when the door is closed, Rose."

The girl gave a galvanic start when she saw Beth poised at the top of the steps. Then, in a colorless voice, she said, "Very well, miss," and retreated to the kitchen.

I'll have to speak to Chris about her, Beth thought. Anyhow, if Martha Mumford was still keeping him, he would not have time to dress for dinner. She went to the study door and knocked. There was no answer. She pushed the door open and looked in. The room was empty.

Seeing the Dutch door swinging ajar, she decided that Chris must have let Mummy out this way and walked to the gate with her. As she turned the handle to close, she saw the gleaming bald head of a man who had been peering above the sill of the dining room window duck out of sight as the man dropped to the ground and slipped away into the shadows. She stood where she was for a moment, a puzzled frown puckering her smooth brow. What on earth was he doing? Someone interested in Rose? She drew farther back into the room, looking through the window. Then the Dutch door opened and Chris stood facing her, his hair tumbled, his breath coming hurriedly as though he had been running.

"Chris, what on earth have you been doing?" she exclaimed. She looked at his knees, at the unmistakable signs of dirt on his trousers.

His eyes followed her glance. "Mussy," he said briefly. "I must change for dinner." And he went quickly out of the room and up the stairs.

When Beth entered the drawing room, the teathings had been cleared away and Anne Bradford, always the first of the family to be dressed for dinner, was glancing idly over the evening paper. Her eyes smiled a welcome.

"Yellow suits you," she said. The smile faded. "Anything wrong?"

Beth glanced behind her and lowered her voice. "That new maid, Rose. This is the second time I've caught her listening at Chris's study door. I just prevented her from going in. She acted scared to death when she saw me watching her. What do you know about the girl?"

Rose, Nan explained, had been in her employ for about a month, coming at the end of the season. Her work was most satisfactory, suspiciously satisfactory, for it was an unprecedented thing to find a maid in the country in the fall who had such a perfect mastery of her trade. She was deft, expert, personally attractive and her English was irreproachable—when she was off guard. She seemed to be making a deliberate effort to talk as she thought a maid was expected to talk.

"I hate to bother Chris about it," she confessed. "He has a lot on his mind lately; something is worrying him and I don't want to add my domestic worries."

"Evelyn?" Beth asked.

Mrs. Bradford shook her head. "I don't think so. It never went deep enough for that." She looked across the room to where Ted sprawled on the couch, reading. The hall clock chimed.

"Ted, dinner in half an hour and you are not dressed. Yes, you must," she laughed in response to an imploring look. "You know that dressing for dinner is one of the few things about which Chris is insistent. He declares that the little amenities of life are more necessary in the country than in the town, so trot along, honey."

The boy rose and stretched his great length till it seemed to his mother that his arms must reach the ceiling.

"What Chris says goes in this house," he admitted good-naturedly. "But when I get married and have a home of my own it will be conducted strictly along the lines of primitive rusticity. Say, that's an impressive phrase: primitive rusticity. I must try it on Smithy, who thinks the vocabulary of the average American college man would shame a foreign child of ten."

His eyes widened as he surveyed Beth. "Whee! A Paris gown, no less. Madam, are you trying to dazzle the eyes of us yokels?—Oho, I know, this is for the benefit of poor old Smithy. It's not fair."

He seized his mother and swung her to the top of the desk. "Make her leave the poor man alone," he said in a hoarse whisper. "He hasn't a chance."

"Theodore." His mother's tone of mock reproof was contradicted by the eyes, so like her boy's, which laughed at him.

"Nan, as a disciplinarian you are an imposter," complained Beth.

Ted lifted his mother carefully down from the desk before he raced up the stairs two at a time, singing as he went. His song rose and fell in the distance, accompanied at times by the thud of a shoe or the sound of running water.

"By no stretch of the imagination can Ted be called the quiet type," Beth laughed.

"I like seeing all that energy," said a voice in the doorway. "It means his strength is flooding back."

"I know," Beth said softly. "It's wonderful to see

how much better he is." She blinked tears from her eyes. "Are you ready for your secretary, Mr. Smith?" she asked gaily. "If you are, bring another chair to the desk, please. I await your orders." She lifted the cover off the small portable machine which Mrs. Bradford used for typing her menus and household orders.

Anne Bradford took the newspaper and curled up in the seat Ted had vacated. Occasionally, she looked over the top of the periodical at the two people at the desk. Beth was absorbed in her task, earnest and enthusiastic as she always was over anything which she undertook. She thought of Ted's nonsense. It would not be difficult for any man to love the girl, she realized, as she studied the beautiful face with its deep, earnest eyes, its red lips and their charming curves, the clear skin with the rose tint in the cheeks, the perfect nose and dimpled chin. The head was crowned with waves of bronze hair and rose from faultless shoulders. Beth sat with her hands poised over the keys, looking up with shining, expectant eyes at the man beside her. His usually inscrutable face was alight with animation. Why—why couldn't Chris see how lovely she was? Dear blind Chris, would the scales ever fall from his eyes?

At the desk Smith began to dictate in a brisk, businesslike way, from notes scrawled on a piece of paper. The first two letters held Beth's attention because, at first, she was awkward at typing, and absorbed in the mechanics. Then, as her work became automatic, her attention wandered, and she observed the hands which had come too close to poison ivy. Her mind drifted while she typed. Poison ivy. But where on earth would he encounter it at the Manor? Every year the first shoots were sprayed and carefully removed. No, there was one place where, with dogged determination to survive, it kept coming back. Where? The place eluded her.

Beth's wayward attention snapped back as the meaning of Smith's dictation struck her.

"Why," she exclaimed, "you are a writer!"

He smiled at her enthusiasm. "Why not?"

"What an exciting career! What books have you written?"

"Not books. Short stories. I can't afford the time that is necessary for a book—yet," he added with a touch of bitterness.

"What kind of stories?" she demanded, her eyes glowing.

There was a pause and then he said reluctantly, "Science fiction. It's a living."

"Oh, I thought from what Ted said that you were a college professor on sabbatical, or whatever they call it."

Unobtrusively he brought the conversation back to the letter and she finished typing it, feeling that in some unintentional way she had been untactful, intruding on his privacy.

At length Smith gathered up the letters she had typed for him.

"That is all, and thank you very much, Miss Gilbert. You have helped tremendously."

Beth dropped a demure curtsy. "I am glad if I gave satisfaction, sir," she answered with exaggerated humility.

With a word to Mrs. Bradford, Smith left the room. They heard him exchange a greeting with Chris, who came in, his hair smooth, in impeccable dinner clothes.

Unexpectedly he spoke to Beth. "What were you doing for Smith?"

"He's a writer, Chris," she began eagerly.

"What were doing for him?" he repeated. There was a little white line about his lips.

"Just typing some letters," Beth said, surprised by the curtness of his tone. "The poor fellow poisoned his hands with ivy and couldn't do it himself."

"He'll have to try. Don't do it again."

The girl's eyes smoldered dangerously.

"Chris," she began, when the telephone rang and Ted came storming down in his tempestuous way to answer it.

"Yes? . . . Sounds fine. By the way, Beth's home. . . . I'll ask her." He turned around to say, "Some friends of Jane Towle's have dropped in and they're planning to dance later. She asked Chris and me and screamed with joy over you being back. Will you go?"

"Love to," the girl said promptly.

Chris shook his head. "Not tonight, Ted. You two kids run along but don't stay out late. You have to work tomorrow, Ted, and for heaven's sake don't try to find out how fast you can drive that new car of yours."

"Ay, ay, sir," the boy said cheerfully.

"Do you think it is safe to let the kids go out alone at night?" Beth asked, when Ted had accepted for them both. Her voice was suspiciously smooth, her cheeks were red, her eyes harbored sparks of indignation.

"Sorry, Beth," Chris laughed. He had quite regained his temper. "I suppose you and Ted will always be kids to me."

"Will we indeed?" There was a new quality in the girl's voice which made Anne Bradford look at her quickly. "Come on, Ted. We must get our bibs and blocks."

After dinner, Chris stood before the fire drinking his coffee. His mother in a chair near him gazed thoughtfully into the blaze.

"It's quiet with the kids gone, isn't it?" he remarked. After a moment's rumination he added, "It is unusual for Beth to misunderstand me. I thought she was rather annoyed when she left."

"She has grown up, Chris. She was probably annoyed at being treated like a child. After all, she has seen a great deal of the world, she has been extraordinarily popular socially; she was really sensational her first season. A number of men have wanted to marry her."

"She can't marry without my consent and approval," he said quickly.

There was a quizzical lift to Nan Bradford's eyebrows. "Do you think it is wise to be so peremptory? You have an enormous influence over Beth but if you issue orders like a tyrant you'll have a rebellion on your hands and I can't say I would blame her."

"A tyrant!" Chris laughed.

"Perhaps," his mother said tentatively, not wanting to force his confidence but eager to show her interest, "you were a shade tyrannical with Evelyn."

Chris shook his head smiling ruefully. "That's about the only reason she didn't give for breaking our engagement."

"She told Julia it was because of Beth."

"Evelyn gave me a lot of good reasons, Mother—keeping Beth here was only one of them. She more than hinted I wanted Beth under my eyes so I could be sure of maintaining control of the Gilbert formula."

"Chris!"

"I know," he said. "It isn't pretty, is it? And there were other things: the fact that people come to me with their troubles and take my attention from her; the fact that I like living in the country and she hates it. Dead and alive, she called it." He set down the empty coffee cup. "They were all good reasons but they weren't the real reason. I feel sure of that."

"And the real reason?"

"Mark Craven," Chris said briefly. "I have a profound conviction that if Mr. Craven had never appeared upon the scene she could have borne up under my fancied neglect, even under having to spend six months a year in the country."

"Who is he, Chris? I've met him several times—Julia insisted on introducing him—but I don't really like him. He is polished, his manners are beyond criticism, and yet—"

Chris's eyebrows shot up. "So Julia introduced him!"

"Yes, he has become quite a constant caller at her house. He was there when she asked me to tea one afternoon. There seems to be hard feeling between Julia and Evelyn because of his attentions. Both of them seem to believe—or want to believe—that they are his real object."

Chris smiled grimly. "Poor Julia," he said. "She hasn't a chance against Evelyn, who is younger and better-looking and—" His lips tightened. "I am sorry Beth was hurt by what Evelyn said. But I don't understand why she let it trouble her. After all, Beth should know how we feel about her. Colonel Jim has always said that she is like you in that—in her understanding, I mean."

His mother made no comment, and after a moment Chris said tentatively, "I wonder why the colonel has never married."

Mrs. Bradford made no reply.

"You and Father and he grew up together, didn't you?"

His mother's lips trembled. She steadied them before she answered, "Yes, I have known him for years. Perhaps—perhaps there was some youthful attachment. One always suspects some girl in the background when a man reaches Jim's age, charming and chivalrous with women but with never a hint of an affair."

"Were you the girl, Mother?"

When she made no answer, Chris went on slowly, "Because I have a message for you from Father. When he knew that he was dying he said, 'Chris, I want your mother to be happy. Jim Haswell has always loved her. He was devoted while I was hovering around other girls, then I suddenly awoke to the beauty and perfection of Anne Seagreave. I was mad with love of her. I would have her. I didn't use the fairest means in cutting out Jim. She knew it—afterwards. She has always been loyal, wonderful, but—I have had a tap on the shoulder; I'll have to leave her. She is a young woman and still lovely. If ever the time comes when you think it should be said, tell her my one wish was for her happiness.' I think, perhaps, the time has come to tell you that."

Anne Bradford rose and brushed her hand across her eyes. For a moment she rested her cheek against his sleeve. "I wish—I wish that every woman had a son like you. Now, I know I am keeping you from your work. Run along. But leave the study door open so I can see you, dear. I'm a spoiled woman. I love to have a man about."

Bradford entered his room and turned on more light as he pulled some papers toward him. High time, he thought, that someone bothered about making his mother happy. She had done enough for other people. And she was wiser about people than he. Certainly she had understood Evelyn Furnas better than he had. He dropped his pen and rested his head on his hand.

He was amazed at the sense of relief he felt now that his engagement was over. Evelyn had hampered and discouraged him in all he had tried to do. He wondered why he had ever become engaged to her. He had drifted into it, following the path of least resistance. Certainly she had meant little to him. Would his pulses ever leap at the sound of a woman's voice? Sometimes he doubted it.

He shook off his thoughts and tackled his accounts once more. He worked intently, then stopped, his pen uplifted. He snapped out the light and cautiously moved the shade at the window. The figure of a man was discernible in the dim light outside. He was stooping over. Then he stood up and flung up his arm. There was a sound of pebbles rattling on the floor of the balcony outside Smith's room. A few moments later stealthy steps descended the stairs and the outside door closed softly. Now there were two shadows where there had been one before.

Chris thrust his hands into the pockets of his coat and stared into space. John Smith, Ted's tutor, was behaving in a most peculiar fashion. Shortly after dinner Chris had seen him steal around the house, had followed him on impulse, and had watched him open the mailbox and look hastily through the letters which were waiting for the postman. It wasn't a case of second thoughts about a letter he had written. He had removed nothing. But he had examined carefully all the letters which Chris had left to be mailed.

He remembered Martha Mumford's question. What,

after all, did he know about Smith? That he was doing a good job for Ted, who admired him greatly. His answer, in reply to Chris's advertisement for a tutor, had filled the bill so well that Chris had not checked up on his references. A fool thing to do, he admitted to himself.

The outside door was flung open and laughing voices filled the hall. Beth and Ted had returned from the party, bringing the freshness and coolness of out of doors with them.

Chris pushed aside his work and went out to join them.

Ted had flung himself down on the couch and was looking at Beth, whistling, ". . . And then my heart stood still."

"Stop it, Ted," the girl implored. "You've kept it up all the way home."

"That," Ted informed his older brother, "is the theme song for the dashing Mark Craven. He took one look at Beth and then his heart stood still. Did he go overboard!"

"Don't be ridiculous," Beth said. "I'm going to bed. Good night."

She went quickly out of the room, avoiding Chris's eyes. He looked after her for a moment in surprise. "And how about Beth?" he asked. "Did she go overboard too?"

Ted scoffed. "You know Beth. Gay and friendly but not swept off her feet. She didn't seem much interested. It was Aunt Julia who was livid. She brought our conquering hero to the Towles' and then he deserted her to trail after Beth with a bemused look in his eyes."

"Why does Julia have to go around with a man like that?" Chris said in annoyance. "He may not be at all the kind of man for Beth to know—particularly if he is interested in Evelyn as she believes."

His mother suppressed a smile at the anxiety in his tone. It wasn't Evelyn, his ex-fiancée, who was arousing his jealousy. "Beth is an exceptionally lovely girl, Chris. There are bound to be men in love with her.

But we can trust her good judgment. She is not easily
misled about people. She knows what is real and
genuine."

"Do you think I should refuse to let him see her?"

At his tone, Ted sat up abruptly, his mouth half
open in surprise.

"Chris," his mother protested, "do you want to spoil
everything? Why is it that you, who can advise every
man, woman and child who comes to see you, seem to
have lost your judgment completely in dealing with
Beth?"

"Still, it's hardly right not to give her some guid-
ance. After all, I'm responsible for her."

His mother strangled back a laugh. "You might
escort her yourself, now and then. You may not be
much use as a partner at your advanced age," she
teased, "but you could make sure that no bold, bad
youth interested her."

"Perhaps I shall," Chris said coolly. "Anyhow, I
intend to get out a bit just to prove that I am not
heartbroken over Evelyn. And, whether she likes it
or not, I am going to keep an eye on Beth."

Ted chuckled. "Beth can look after herself."

Footsteps raced down the stairs and Beth stood in
the drawing room doorway, her face white. "Chris,"
she panted, "someone has searched my room."

"Searched! You mean robbed?" he said incredu-
lously.

"No, searched," she repeated. "Nothing was taken
but everything is in a mess—suitcases, dresser drawers, closets, desk, everything."

"But why?"

"I don't know," she cried, "but it's not the first time.
This has happened to me over and over for months,
in England and Scotland and France and Holland
and Switzerland. Only—I thought I'd be safe—here."

V

Dan-ger. . . . Dan-ger. . . . Danger. . . . The windshield wipers kept up their monotonous whisper. *Dan-ger.*

Chris, holding the car down to a low speed, drove through the heavy rain, his eyes on the wet road ahead, but his nerves throbbing with that reiterated whisper: *Dan-ger.*

In the days since Beth Gilbert's unexpected return from Europe he had lost weight and his face was drawn from sleeplessness. He still recalled his ward's startled eyes when she had raced down the stairs to announce that her room had had been searched. Not only that. She had been followed in Europe and her belongings searched again and again.

Over and over, he had attempted to reassure himself. In the first place, Beth might have imagined that furtive pursuit through Europe. On the other hand, she had certainly not imagined the confusion in which he had found her room that night when he had raced up the stairs with Ted close at his heels. It had been a scene of chaos. And yet nothing had been taken. A string of fine pearls lay untouched in a dresser drawer; eighty dollars in bills had been left in her handbag.

Possibly in Europe she might have been mistaken for someone else, someone carrying a document, an incriminating letter, something of vital importance. But there could be no possibility of mistaken identity here. Everyone in the community knew her.

So what was left? Chris faced it grimly. What was left was the Gilbert formula. But, if anyone believed Gilbert had left it with his daughter, that meant that whoever had knocked him down—face it, Chris; whoever had killed him—that night two years before had

41

failed to get the formula. Or were there two different people at work?

The only thing that was clear, unmistakable, was the fact that Beth was in danger. After days of anguished thought and sleepless night during which he watched Beth's door to make sure that she was safe, Chris had decided to put the whole problem up to his mother's oldest friend, Colonel Jim Haswell. Colonel Jim's judgment was sound, his advice would be worth consulting, and he was utterly trustworthy.

Perhaps, too, Colonel Jim would be able to influence Beth. In his anxiety about her Chris was well aware that he had been both peremptory and unreasonable. He checked up on every place she went, on every person she visited, on every telephone call she received. No wonder Beth, normally sweet and good-tempered, was exasperated by an interference which seemed to her completely unreasonable. If he could have enlisted his mother's aid it might have helped but he could not bear causing her worry and alarm. Nor could be bring himself to tell Beth the truth.

Why frighten her when he was able to protect her? Why shadow her days by telling her that the man responsible for her father's death was still at large? Why disturb her by explaining that if the formula were found, if it proved to be all Gilbert had believed, if it were manufactured—so many ifs—she would become a fabulously wealthy woman?

He had listened to her account of Rose's odd behavior but had declined to dismiss the maid. If she was acting for someone it would be better to keep her where she could be under observation.

Dan-ger, the windshield wipers whispered. *Danger*. Chris forced himself to relax, to ease his tight grip on the wheel. No one would hurt Beth. It was inconceivable that anyone would hurt Beth. Self-reliant as she was, filled with high courage and gallantry of spirit, there was, nonetheless, something about her that made men want to protect her.

But what man? Chris asked himself suddenly. Who is good enough for her? Does she like this man Craven? Heaven knows, he seems to be telephoning at all hours of the day since he met her, sending lavish flowers—much too lavish to be in good taste—asking to see her. According to rumor, he was a man of vast wealth; according to Julia, he had great charm; certainly he had been the reason for Evelyn Furnas's broken engagement. Craven had had more to offer than Chris. But, apparently, Evelyn had miscalculated for Craven had not made the offer. Instead, he had transferred his attentions to Beth Gilbert.

Chris tried to look at the matter sensibly, with detachment. After all, Craven appeared from all accounts to be an exceptional man. If Beth wanted to marry him he would be amply able to look after her, to protect her from the danger that threatened. If Beth wanted to marry him—

Chris found himself wincing away from the idea. Beth married to someone else. Beth, who had trotted at his heels since she was a lanky child of fourteen, who had ridden over the estate at his side every chance she could get. Her judgment had been excellent. It was more than a gay companion who had ridden beside him; it was a wise counselor. She had often urged clemency when his decision had been too harsh. She had, as Jim Haswell frequently pointed out, a fine sense of human values. Indeed, she was as good as Colonel Jim at sizing up a man. He had often hired employees on her recommendation and had never regretted her choice. Her understanding of people went deep.

Chris stopped his car with a suddenness that took it into a skid. He straightened it out. The girl who was trudging along the road stopped and looked up. The rain was pelting down, her sweater was soaked, and water dripped from the brim of her soft hat.

"Why are you out in this rain, Beth?" her guardian demanded sharply.

She peered up at him from eyes alight with mutiny. The rain had stung the color into her cheeks and chin. Her hair rioted in little damp curls about her face.

"Taking a sun bath, of course," she retorted.

"Hop in!"

"Really, Chris, you snap orders like a marine sergeant."

"Please, Beth," he implored, "get in out of the rain. Or shall I come out for you? That's a good child."

"Christopher Bradford, if you don't stop calling me a child—"

"Miss Gilbert, on my bended knees—"

She laughed and got into the car. "Don't scold any more," she begged him. "I'm disgusted. This is my brand-new sweater, for which I exchanged a good slice of my month's allowance, and it is ruined."

"Perhaps we could stretch the allowance to a new one," he suggested.

"Chris, that's one thing I've been wanting to ask you. About my allowance. Did my father—have I a right—is there any money of my own? I'm not living on your money, am I?"

"Your father provided for you," Chris assured her. "I thought you knew that. And I'm ready, you know," he added jokingly, "to make an accounting of your estate when you marry. But what made you think of that? Would you mind so terribly if the money were mine?"

She made no reply.

He bent forward to look into her face but she turned her head away.

"What is it, Beth?" he asked gently.

"It's you," she burst out rebelliously. "Ever since I've come home you've given orders; you've demanded an accounting for my time and my friends and—and—"

"Forgive me," he said, "and try to trust me a little. One of these days I'll explain the whole thing."

"When I've grown up, I suppose."

"As soon as I can. I promise that. I haven't meant to be arbitrary or disagreeable. But you're too precious to be jeopardized, Beth."

Something in the man's quiet voice made Beth's breath catch in her throat.

"Where are you taking me, Chris? I'm wet and cold."

"Sorry. I'm going to Colonel Jim's to discuss some business. His housekeeper will let you have some dry clothes and Colonel Jim will give you some hot tea."

Mrs. Altman, Colonel Haswell's housekeeper, received them with motherly concern. She had managed the old colonial house for the colonel's mother and now ruled its present master with a rod of iron. As it was a kindly rod and wielded only for his comfort, the colonel tried to bear it as befitted an officer and a gentleman.

The housekeeper rang a bell before she hurried the girl off to a guest room. A stocky butler with massive shoulders, a deeply lined face and sleek brown hair met them at the stairs.

"Stone, serve tea in the living room at once. Telephone the stables for Colonel Haswell. Tell him that Miss Gilbert and Mr. Bradford are here."

For a fleeting instant the butler looked at Beth with startled curiosity and then he turned quietly and went away.

As she peeled off wet garments and tried to dry her hair, Beth inquired, "How long have you had Stone? I don't remember seeing him before."

The housekeeper's head was in the depths of a chest. Her voice was muffled and punctured with short breaths as she pawed through the contents.

"About three weeks—he dropped out of the sky—he applied for the place—the very day after—Fleming gave notice."

"Had he worked around here before?"

"Miss Beth, the colonel took him without so much as a reference, because he was so glad to get a butler at this time of year. I advised him against it; you know the Haswell silver could never be replaced. But I must say Stone has tried very hard, and though he doesn't seem to have had a great deal of experience he learns quickly."

She emerged from the chest, her face flushed from exertion. "Here, put these on, Miss Beth. They belonged to Colonel Haswell's sister. They ought to fit you for she was about your size. Your clothes will be dry by the time you have finished tea. But I am afraid those shoes are hopeless."

"What dainty things they are!" the girl exclaimed. She slipped into a blue silk kimono heavily embroidered with a flock of storks, thrust her feet into matching slippers, combed out the damp curls into soft waves and smiled approval at the vision which confronted her in the mirror.

"I could care for myself in this pale blue," she laughed.

Mrs. Altman looked her admiration. "I guess you're not the only one who could care for you," she observed dryly. "While you're serving tea perhaps Mr. Chris will give me some advice. The cook's boy is in trouble and Mr. Chris will know just how to handle him."

"More problems for Chris," the girl thought as she went down the stairs.

At the living room door she paused and looked in. Chris, perched on a corner of the table, was talking earnestly to Colonel Haswell. The latter, stretched out in a deep, softly cushioned chair, frowned as he listened. The colonel was a man in the mid-fifties with a stern Websterian face and iron-gray hair which was beginning to thin at the temples. His eyes were deep blue, keen as blades under the overhanging brows, but Beth knew that they could be very tender. He had made the army his profession until five years before, when he had resigned in order to be with his mother during her last years. That an inactive life was irksome to him his friends could not doubt, but he had made his mother feel that he loved it and had plunged enthusiastically into the town interests, Julia Seagreave in her italicized, sentimental way had likened him to a crusader.

The room reflected its owner. The wonderfully cushioned couch, and chairs into which one could sink to unplumbed depths, were luxuriously tempting. There was a blazing fire on the hearth before which two beagles dozed. On one side of the fireplace hung the Revolutionary Haswell's certificate of membership in the Cincinnati; below it a later Haswell's commission in the Federal Army, signed in full, *Abraham Lincoln*. The yellow sash of a cavalry sword made a blotch of light against the dark wall. There was a glow at the girl's heart as she thought of the men who had lived and fought. She was flamingly patriotic and loved Colonel Jim not only for his unfailing tenderness to her but for the record behind him.

She was about to run into the room with a laughing comment when something in the attitude of the two men, something engrossed, tense, serious, checked her. She heard the murmur of words: ". . . formula . . . danger . . ."

What formula? she wondered. What danger? Then it occurred to her that she was loitering outside the door like Rose and she went in quickly.

"Come in, my dear," Colonel Jim called in welcome as he rose to his feet to greet her. "I was afraid that wetting had hurt you but no one would worry about your health after seeing you as you are now. You positively glow. And Chris was worrying about the effect of a little rain on you."

"Naturally," Beth laughed, "old, settled-down people like Chris are afraid of the weather. I sometimes wonder, Colonel Jim, whether Chris hasn't forgotten his own youth."

She smiled tormentingly at Bradford. To her unutterable surprise, instead of parrying her thrust, he turned abruptly away and took up his position in front of the fire. The girl looked at him wonderingly, then up at the man who still held her two hands in his. He met the question in her eyes gravely.

"Chris has a lot on his mind," he explained.

As Beth seated herself within the glow of the blaze, the dogs laid their forepaws on her lap and tried to lick her face, then they settled on either side of her like sentinels. Stone entered and set the tea tray on a small table before her. The dogs thumped their tails furiously at sight of the butler and looked up at him wistfully, their great soft ears dangling like earrings, but they made no move to desert the girl.

"Cream?" Beth asked as she held the silver jug suspended above a cup.

There was a stir in the hall, then a voice.

"How are you, Haswell? You asked me to come in some day and here I am. This infernal weather drove me out in search of companionship."

With an exclamation of pleasure Beth held out her hand to the owner of the voice as he entered the room. "This is a nice surprise. Did you rain down too, Mr. Craven?"

"Good luck to find you here, Miss Gilbert. That rain cloud had a silver lining all right."

Not luck, Chris thought. Craven knew she was here. He was startled by the ferocity of the spasm of jealousy he felt and made an effort to keep his naked hostility from his face as Beth introduced the two men.

"Mr. Craven, I don't believe you know Christopher Bradford, my guardian."

Guardian, Chris thought. That's a nasty, middle-aged word for you.

Mark Craven was large and blond, with the ruddiness of skin that goes with perfect health. His eyes were strangely colorless; his hands, in spite of the fact that they were cared for, were faintly repellent, with a suspicion of flabbiness about them, the fingers slightly cushioned at the tips.

Beth observed those hands as the two men greeted each other, her gaze lingering for a moment on the strong, finely shaped hands of her guardian. Why, she wondered, when Chris could be so charming and gracious, was he frosty, almost brusque now? Was it because Evelyn had broken her engagement on account of this man? With her infallible social sense, she endeavored to counteract his stiffness by leaning forward and smiling in the warmest, most friendly fashion.

"Tea, Mr. Craven?"

"Thank you. Strong with no trimmings, please."

With flattering haste Craven drew a chair beside the girl. Mischievously aware of Bradford's aloofness and disapproval, Beth exerted herself to entertain the colonel's guest. She was vibrant with life and fun and sweetness. Craven's colorless eyes flamed into lamps of light. Their expression made the girl vaguely uncomfortable, but she did find the man interesting. At least, he knew that she had grown up.

"When," he pleaded, "are you going to let me call on you?"

"When you like," she smiled.

Stone stood in the doorway. "Mrs. Seagreave, Mr. Theodore Bradford," he announced.

The young widow swept forward and laid one hand on Haswell's arm. "How are you, Jim? Dear Chris, I called the Manor and asked Nan where you were. She said you had come here so I asked Ted to be an angel and pick me up and bring me along. Mr. Craven—what a coincidence that we should meet here. It's really absurd the way it happens so often. Something in our stars, perhaps."

Craven rose to bow over her hand but he did not appear to notice the invitation in her voice. His eyes returned to the girl who presided over the tea tray.

Julia Seagreave's face flushed, "Beth, why on earth are you dressed like that? Foreign customs, I suppose. Anne would be simply horrified if she knew, *chagrined to death*. In a small community, my dear, you are apt to start people talking by that sort of thing."

A cyclone of anger which left her breathless for a moment swept over the girl. Before she could speak in her own defense, Chris said tranquilly, "We thought Colonel Haswell's housekeeper provided a charming substitute for Beth's wet clothes. She was caught in the rain and I brought her here so that she could change before she caught cold."

Beth's anger drained away. She looked at the older woman with an amused light in her eyes. "If my guardian is satisfied, all is well. Will you have tea?"

Mrs. Seagreave sank into a chair near Craven's.

"Yes, of course. Mr. Craven, do talk to me. I haven't seen you for *years*."

Craven looked from Julia to Beth, his face expressionless. "Let me take Mrs. Seagreave's cup," he said, presented it to the widow, and returned to Beth's side. The color deepened in Julia's face.

"Chris," she complained, "you must explain my income tax to me. I am a *child* when it comes to business." She turned back to Craven, trying desperately to draw his attention away from Beth. "You know, I depend on Chris for *everything*. He's like a big brother."

"I should think he was more like a son," Ted interposed.

"Ted," Beth whispered, "that was unkind."

"What do you call what she has been saying to you?" he answered angrily.

The widow rallied gallantly. "Chris," she said peremptorily, and he sat down near her. "Jim Haswell, do join us. I am simply *crazed* over the obscurities of my tax."

"Why not ask Beth?" Ted said mischievously. "Chris has her make out her own and his too. She's a bear at figures."

Beth grasped his arm and pulled him down beside her. "Ted, you are simply flinging me to the lions."

"I'll leave you with the great Craven," he whispered. "If Evelyn could only see him now! He's practically eating you up with his eyes."

With Julia's jealousy, Chris's coldness and restraint, and Craven's embarrassing admiration, the party was no longer amusing, and Beth, with a murmured excuse, slipped away to the guest room, where Mrs. Altman was waiting with her dry clothes.

As she returned to the living room, Craven, whom Julia had cornered at last and to whom she was talking eagerly, one hand on his arm as though fearing he would escape her, stepped forward. He was not the kind of man to be easily checked in anything he wanted.

"Miss Gilbert," he said quickly, "do let me take you home. It won't do to have you caught in the rain again. Anyhow, I'd like to know what you think of my car."

"I've seen it, Mr. Craven, and it looks wonderful," Beth began when Chris cut in.

"Much obliged to you, Craven, but my ward is going with me. Ready, Beth?" He moved toward the door without waiting for her answer.

Beth's eyes glowed rebelliously as she held out her hand to Haswell.

"Good-by, Colonel Jim! Good afternoon, Julia! Mr. Craven, perhaps someday you will drive me in that wonderful car of yours."

"Someday I certainly shall," he assured her. He ignored the waiting Bradford while he held her for several moments in laughing conversation.

The torrential downpour continued. The afternoon light had disappeared and the road was quite dark. Bradford drove carefully. It was comfortable in the closed car, shut in from the storm with Chris at her side. Beth let her head drop back against the seat with a sigh of sheer content. After the tensions of the tea party this was a refuge, this was peace. She felt her resentment at Chris's cavalier treatment oozing away and made a clutch for it.

"Chris, it's not fair for you to dictate to me as you do," she protested. "I couldn't make a scene about it in public; it would have made us both ridiculous. But, after all, how did you know but what I was longing to ride home with Mr. Craven in that stunning car of his?"

"Were you?"

"Well, I—"

"Were you?"

"Must you be such a piece of Scotch granite?" she said in exasperation. "As you know perfectly well, I wasn't; I'd rather be with you and Nan and Ted than anyone else on earth. But you might at least let me speak for myself."

"Do you mean that, Beth?"

"Of course I do."

He drew a quick breath of relief before he said lightly, "Because—because my advanced age makes me a safe companion, I presume."

She laughed, tucking her hand under his arm in friendly companionship. "Because you are a good companion, Chris."

VI

Above the insistent ringing of the telephone caroled Ted's exuberant young voice.

I am the monarch of the sea
The ruler of the Queen's Navee!

"Ted, please," implored his mother, as she picked up the telephone and held out a restraining hand to the boy who came marching into the room in time to the tune he was warbling at the top of his fresh clear voice. "I can't even hear myself think above that racket."

"Racket," he complained in an injured voice, tiptoed elaborately across the room, made himself comfortable astride a chair, leaned his elbows securely on the back of it and whispered hoarsely, "Jeer on, cruel female. Thou hast stilled this marvelous voice forever."

His mother laughed and blew a kiss to him before she turned back to the telephone.

"Yes? . . . Oh, Evelyn. . . . Why, I—" for a moment Mrs. Bradford seemed to be at a loss. Then she said reluctantly, "Of course, you may come, if you care to under the circumstances. . . . You should know Chris too well to believe he is capable of harboring any resentment of that kind. . . ."

Anne Bradford's face whitened and Ted was beside her in one stride. She gripped his sleeve with a shaking hand.

"Yes, I have met Mr. Craven, but I don't really know him. . . . *Refuse* to know him? Not at all. You may bring him, if you like. I had no idea he was interested in old houses. . . . Yes, the antiquarians are all enthusiastic about the Manor. Very well, we shall expect you both at eight o'clock."

Anne Bradford put down the telephone and turned to her son in distress. He was perched on the desk beside her, one knee clasped in his arms.

"What's the idea of Evelyn coming here?" he glowered.

His mother made a helpless gesture. "I don't like it either," she admitted, "but what could I do? After all, she knows we always plan for informal dinner guests on Wednesdays. I could not refuse to see her. But I don't understand it."

"She's trying to get Chris back," Ted hazarded.

"Perhaps," his mother said doubtfully, "though—you see, dear, she asked to bring Mr. Craven with her. It seems he is eager to see the Manor—"

"And Beth," Ted interpolated.

There was a puzzled frown between his mother's brows. "Evelyn would never be so eager to bring him here for that reason. I wish I knew what they really wanted."

"It's just possible," Ted said, "they want different things. And, if you ask me, they are both the kind of people to go after what they want, and Craven is much more intelligent than Evelyn about getting it. Perhaps she wants to please him, but I'll wager Craven is interested in Beth. You haven't seen them together, Mother. His eyes never leave her."

"You don't like him, do you?"

"Well, he's not equal to Chris," Ted acknowledged, "but he's not a bad sort. He simply reeks of success, that's all. The-world-is-mine type. That's what puzzles me about him."

"What do you mean?"

"Well, can you see a man of his financial importance, with a lot of weighty matters to handle, hanging around the country like this, week after week? He's not one of those tired businessmen getting a rest. He's in the pink. I don't make it out." He grinned at her. "Evelyn certainly knows how to get around you.

All anyone has to do is to praise this house or your boys and you are wax in their hands."

Anne Bradford looked up from under her long lashes with a glint of laughter in her eyes. "At least, you might put my boys first, mightn't you?" The smile left her eyes. "Do you think Chris will be troubled by Evelyn's coming?"

"Nuts," Ted said bluntly. "Now that old Chris has the blinkers off, he's wise to her tricks. He must see the difference between Evelyn and Beth. Now I ask you—would anyone look at the Duchess when Slim is around?" He looked at his watch. "I've got to hustle. Smithy's waiting to tackle Spanish with me. How that man makes me slave."

He lifted his voice.

I am the monarch of the sea
The ruler of the Queen's Navee!

Anne Bradford sat motionless as the notes of the boy's song rose and fell in the distance. What a happy, loyal, comforting soul he was. She smiled as she remembered his indictment of her. It was true, she admitted to herself, she was as wax in the hands of one who expressed appreciation of her sons. But she would not, she vowed, be wax in Evelyn's slim, ruthless hands. She touched a button in the wall. While she waited she drew on her gloves, her mind far removed from their immaculate whiteness.

"You rang, Madam?"

Anne Bradford looked up. "Yes, Rose. I am going out. Tell Cook we shall have two extra guests at dinner, Miss Furnas and Mr. Craven." She added quickly, "What is the matter? Are you ill?"

The maid struggled to smile.

"No, madam, I have a headache, that's all. I have not been out for several days. If I get my table ready early, may Kate take my place while I go out? I am sure that I could do my work better if I have a walk in the fresh air."

"Certainly, Rose. I know that I can depend upon you to have everything in readiness." As the tutor paused for a moment in the doorway, peering myopically through thick lenses, she said, "Mr. Smith, won't you join us for dinner tonight?"

"Thank you, Mrs. Bradford, it would be a pleasure. Unfortunately I have another engagement."

"Oh? I am glad you have made some friends here. You have confined yourself so closely for Ted's sake, I was afraid you would be lonely." As the tutor stood awkwardly in the hallway, without reply, she dismissed him with a pleasant smile. "We shall miss you. Rose, arrange your table early so you can have a long walk in this glorious air. It ought to blow the cobwebs from your brain and the worries from your heart. I suspect you do have worries."

Mrs. Bradford remembered Beth's statement that the maid had been eavesdropping outside Chris's study. No such behavior had ever been tolerated at the Manor, but Chris, for reasons of his own, had asked her not to dismiss the girl. Anyhow, something in the haggard face touched Anne Bradford's heart. The troubled young never left her unmoved. She asked impulsively, "Can I help?"

"No—no, madam. I thank you but—"

"I am not trying to force your confidence," Mrs. Bradford said quickly. "But if ever I can help, come to me. I feel that everyone who lives under the Manor roof has a claim on my sympathy. And then my own youth is not so far behind but that I can remember some of its tragedies."

"Madam—I—"

"I understand. Bring my fur coat to the car. I won't put it on yet."

While the maid was gone Chris came out of his study. "Where's Beth?" he demanded.

"She went out somewhere," Anne answered vaguely.

"You don't know where?" There was a sharp note in her son's voice that made Anne arch her brows in surprise.

"I didn't ask her," she said quietly. "She merits some degree of privacy, Chris. You seem to forget that lately, and it isn't like you."

"I know," he admitted. "Sorry, Mother. I'll try to watch it." He hovered uncertainly in the doorway. "She hasn't been doing any more typing for Smith, has she?"

"Really, Chris," his mother protested.

For a moment he looked at her, running his fingers through his hair, then he turned quickly, went back into the study and closed the door. In a minute Rose appeared with the fur coat and Anne, after reminding her to take a walk, went out.

The maid waited at the front entrance until her mistress nodded to her from behind the glistening windows of the car, then entered the house and closed the door. She leaned back against it, looking unseeingly up at the face of the tall clock that ticked so solemnly and warningly. To her excited fancy it seemed to say: *Tell her! Tell her! Tell her!*

With a little shiver Rose brushed her hand impatiently across her eyes and stole softly through the hall into the living room. How still it was. Mr. Ted was at work in the breakfast room at the other end of the house. Mr. Chris was in his study. She must telephone, she must. If she used the phone in the pantry the other servants might hear. The living room phone tempted her.

She looked furtively about, then crouched in a chair. Outside the window a dry birch cracked with a suddenness which sent the girl leaping half out of her chair. She listened with her hand on her heart and then picked up the telephone and dialed a number.

Suppose he should not be there? But he must be, she must speak to him. She could not endure the intolerable ache at her heart another day. While she listened to the ringing of the phone her eyes roved about the great room. Over the mantel hung a portrait of Mrs. Bradford. The face was young, charming, yet with a touch of wistfulness about the lips which was more noticeable now. She had been very kind, very sympathetic; but could a woman who had known only luxury all her life understand the temptations which might beset a girl less fortunately placed? Surely not. The risk was too great.

How ghostly the house was in its silence. She could hear the ticking of the hall clock, pounding out the suggestion: *Tell her! Tell her! Tell her!*

Then the ringing stopped and a voice spoke.

"It's Rose," she said quickly. . . . "I must see you. Meet me between five and six at the same place. . . . But I *do* have something to report. That's why I called. . . . I think it's what you wanted. . . . All right. Good-by."

She put the telephone down gently with a quick sigs of relief. Then, as a hand touched her shoulder, she caught her breath in a strangled gasp that was almost a cry. For a moment her heart seemed to stiffen into stillness. Little icy thrills crawled through her veins. Then she looked up. Christopher Bradford stood behind her. How much had he heard? What would her end of the conversation mean to him?

"I—I was telephoning."

He stopped her labored explanation with a wave of his hand. This was not the Mr. Chris whom the servants adored, it was a stern, keen-eyed man whose look seemed to probe her secret thoughts. Strange to be afraid of Mr. Chris.

"Rose," he said, "next time you have a message of a private nature to send, be sure you have all the lines in the house at your disposal." Before she could summon up a word he had gone.

The girl stared blindly after him. So he had listened on his extension! How much harm had she done? Would she dare keep her appointment? Had she blundered irretrievably? Well, if she had, she would have to take her punishment. Perhaps that would be better, after all, than to continue to live in this nightmare of fear. Even if the worst happened, it would be almost a relief to have nothing more to dread.

She dropped her head on her arms, huddling deeper into the chair. Every day she seemed to be more hopelessly entangled in the mesh that had been spread to catch her. How had it started anyhow? Her own weakness had been responsible for her first mistake; the second had been a result of trying to set right the first. Now nothing could be right again. Well, there was nothing to do now but to go on—to whatever end was to come, and she no longer believed that the end would be bright for her.

Rose dragged herself wearily out to the kitchen to tell the cook that there would be two extra guests for dinner and to ask Kate to relieve her for a couple of hours.

"Sure I will," the second maid answered, busy over a pan of crisp green lettuce. "Get out of doors. You look as though you were about all in. What's troubling ye?"

"Nothing," Rose said listlessly.

The second maid gave her a shrewd but kindly look. "If I was taking off a couple of hours now," she said casually, "and had something on my mind, I'd take it straight to Martha Mumford at her waffle shop. She's a great one for patching up love affairs that get sort of frayed."

Rose looked at the serene, unruffled face of the buxom girl. "I haven't a love affair, either frayed or whole," she said bitterly. "Anyhow, I tried to keep her out of here one day. I didn't know how the family felt about her. She'd hold it against me."

"Oh, go along wid ye! Mumford's got a temper like the flare of fat drippin' from chops on the range fire, but she don't hold nothin' against anyone, does she, Cook?"

"No, she don't. You go ahead an' ask her anything you want. How many did ye say was coming for dinner?"

Rose almost forgot her personal problems while she arranged the table. It was a delight to the beauty-loving girl to handle the old silver, fragile glass and rare china. When she had placed the bowl of pink carnations in the center she buried her face for a moment in the blossoms and inhaled their fragrance greedily. While there were flowers in the world to touch and smell, she need not wholly despair. Whatever happened to her, the world would still be beautiful.

When Martha Mumford decided that she wanted a home of her own, Anne Bradford, who knew human nature as well as she knew the flowers in her lovely garden, was convinced that the woman would be unhappy without some definite work, something into which she could throw herself heart and soul. So she conceived the idea of setting her up in a waffle shop.

In a short time the little white house with its swinging sign had acquired a fame that enticed motorists from far and near. There were trim maids to serve the food and a boy to help the proprietor in the kitchen. Martha had refused to add afternoon tea to her program, and she was rigid in her determination that the waffle shop should close promptly at five o'clock. After that hour her cosy back sitting room, with its outlook upon the apple orchard and its tea table before the fire, became the rendezvous of many of the young people of the town.

Martha Mumford was rather contemptuous of her contemporaries. She claimed that they came to her for advice, never told her the whole truth of the matter under advisement, went away and did just what they had intended to do all along.

But the youngsters were different. They brought their hopes and fears, their doubts and temptations. Many a distorted view had been brought into focus, many a girl saved from the tragic mistake of marrying a man to reform him, many a boy started on the right trail because Martha Mumford laid down the law to him and then lent him money with which to make a fresh start.

There were people who laughed at her because she had a habit of starting her advice by drawing an analogy to a movie which she had recently seen. But she was wiser than she knew; when she established a parallel between a young shop-girl and a current movie star she raised the girl's problems from the prosaic to the glamorous, endowed a simple life with drama, and frequently made it easier for the girl to make a necessary and difficult sacrifice of immediate wants to future welfare because the beautiful actress had moved her to tears by making the same decision. Yes, Mummy was wise. She helped the young to keep their feet on the ground and at the same time enabled them to give their lives color and beauty. Doing the right thing never needed to be humdrum, she declared. It could be made exciting and daring and challenging if you just knew how to go about it.

Now that the day's work was done, the kitchen spotless, and the girls had gone home, she bustled about energetically as she prepared her simple supper and set it in front of the fire in the sitting room. With the evening paper in her hand she adjusted her spectacles and settled back in her armchair, scanning the headlines between sips of tea and nibbles of toast. This was her hour of relaxation and she enjoyed it to the utmost.

And then through the window drifted a familiar odor, one she had noticed several times before, the scent of an Egyptian cigarette. She dropped the paper onto her lap and looked thoughtfully over it. She sniffed. It was the same scent, no doubt about it.

After a moment's hesitation she extinguished the light and moved cautiously to the window that looked out on the orchard and the lonely road beyond. Instinctively, she found her eyes searching for the figure she had seen several times before, pacing back and forth in the shadow of the trees. Yes, there he was, a man with his hat pulled low.

Something had attracted his attention. Had he become aware of her standing silently at the window? No, he was moving cautiously from tree to tree, working his way toward the front of the house. With her heart fluttering, Martha Mumford stalked him, moving from room to room, from window to window, watching.

As she reached the waffle shop at the front of the cottage, facing on the street, she saw him flatten himself against the side of the building. What was he waiting for?

Beth! Martha's eyes saw the girl coming swiftly along the street, head up, hands thrust deep into the pockets of a green sport coat. Beth and the stranger! It couldn't be.

The man was fumbling in his pocket now; he held something in his hands. He struck three matches in quick succession.

As the matches flared in the twilight, Beth turned her head instinctively. The man started toward her. Beth stood stock-still, startled. Then, as the man continued to approach, she ran at top speed toward the waffle shop, the man thudding close behind.

Martha had the door open before Beth reached it, and as the girl stumbled over the sill, she banged the door shut and bolted it. For a moment the only sound in the room was the girl's panting for breath. Then there was another sound, footsteps on gravel, running away from the house.

"Well," Beth gasped, "lucky—for me—you were—there."

"I'd been watching him for a long time," Martha told her. "I've seen that man loitering around here before."

"But what—does he want?"

"Come in and sit down, child, and catch your breath before you try to talk." The old woman led the girl into the living room and pushed her gently into her own favorite chair. "He's been meeting Rose out there in my orchard. I think he mistook you for her."

"Rose!" Beth sat up alertly. "Something's very wrong with Rose, Mummy." She told the old woman about the two occasions when she had found the girl eavesdropping in front of Chris's door.

"Did you tell Chris?"

"Yes, I did, but he's so odd lately. He refused to fire her. And he didn't want me to mention it. You know, Mummy, I've always suspected that it was

Rose who went through my room that night I came home."

Mumford shook her head. "I saw that room before it was put to rights. No woman, especially no trained maid, did that. That was a man's work."

"But why, Mummy? What do people think I have?"

The old woman studied the girl's glowing face. Young, lovely, candid—she was all those things. But the eyes were level, the mouth firm, the chin had character and determination. It occurred to the old woman that if Rose had had a chin like that she would not go around looking like a scared rabbit.

"I think," she said, "someone is looking for the Gilbert formula."

"Why?"

Millions," Martha Mumford said grimly. "A fortune. There was a movie I saw not long ago about a man who invented something. No one knew about it but his young assistant—Beth, child, did you ever know Larry Sergent, your father's assistant?"

Beth shook her head. "Father never let me go to his laboratory and he never discussed his work with me. In fact, I barely saw him, he was so engrossed in it." For a moment her eyes were starry with tears.

"Anyone ever ask you about your father's work?" Martha demanded. "Have people seemed interested in it since you returned home?"

Beth shook her head again. "No, but that's natural enough. After all, for six years before father died, I lived at the Manor. He hardly ever even visited me. I don't mean to complain. The Bradfords have been all that a real family could possibly have been; they still are. Though Chris—Chris is getting so—so dictatorial it makes me furious. If he had his way I'd hardly leave the house except when he can escort me, and yet if I waited for him to do that I'd never go out. And even in the house—why he was angry when I did some typing for poor Mr. Smith."

"What's so poor about him?" Martha demanded.

"He poisoned his hands with ivy and couldn't use them."

"And where would he get into ivy around a place like the Manor?"

"He didn't say. I wondered too. There used to be a place where it kept growing up—I got it there once myself—only I can't remember where it was."

"What do you think of Mr. Smith?"

"I hardly know. I've seen very little of him. Ted thinks he is wonderful, though a bit too strict." Beth laughed. "He would think anyone too strict who kept him working as hard as Mr. Smith does."

Beth glanced at her watch. "Heavens, I must go back to the Manor. Chris will probably have a fit because I slipped out of the house without saying where I was going. It's a wonder, considering how young and helpless he thinks I am, he doesn't put me in a play pen."

Martha chuckled. "So far as I can make out, you've been doing a lot of going out. People are gossiping in the waffle shop about this Mr. Craven and the way he has fallen for you."

Beth gave a mock sigh of ecstasy. "Now there is a man," she declared, "who knows I have grown up. He doesn't order me around. He notices me. He says flattering things about my dresses, and he hangs on every word I speak, and—believe it or not, Mummy— he thinks I am as beautiful as a movie star."

Martha Mumford's face darkened with indignation. "I declare, just when I think you have some sense, you talk like that about a little flattery. Nothing's so cheap. Why the whole of that man Craven isn't worth Chris's little finger." She did not observe that Beth was struggling to keep from laughing. "Do you see him often?"

"Let's see," Beth said, pretending to count, "three— no, four times this week. Do you think he is neglecting me?"

Martha's indignation faded and a reluctant smile crossed her wrinkled face. "For a moment I almost believed your nonsense."

Beth's smile was tremulous. "Did you really think, Mummy," she said softly, "anyone could compare with Chris? Just the same, it is nice to be noticed by somebody."

There was a timid rap at the outside door. Martha got to her feet. In a moment Beth heard her open the door and say, "Good evening, Rose."

"Oh, Mrs. Mumford," the girl began breathlessly, "I came—" She stepped into the room and saw Beth, who was observing her wonderingly. The color drained out of her face. "I—I had some time off. I thought, it was so dark, Miss Beth might like to have me walk home with her."

"Thanks, Rose," Beth said, "but someone is calling for me."

"Well, then—" The girl backed out awkwardly and so quickly that her departure was almost like flight.

"But why—" Beth began.

Martha Mumford stood at the window, watching thoughtfully as the girl melted into the shadows. "I don't know why she came," she said slowly, "but I know it wasn't for you. It is impossible to see you from outside the window. She never knew you were here until she stepped inside the room."

VII

As the two women stared at each other, there were quick footsteps sounding on the walk, and a sharp rat-tat-tat followed.

Mrs. Mumford beamed. "That's Chris. He always raps like that."

She bustled to the door and threw it wide.

"Well, Chris, I'm as proud as a queen to see you!"

Bradford took her wrinkled hand between his two brown ones. "It's good to see you, Mummy. How is business? Is Beth here? Oh, there you are."

His face lighted up with such relief when he saw her that Beth looked at him in surprise.

"Come for Beth, have you?" the old woman commented. "About time."

Beth gave a gurgle of laughter. "What flattery! I had no idea you were so anxious to get rid of me."

There was no answering laughter in Mrs. Mumford's face. " 'Member the man with the three matches I was telling you about?" she asked Chris. As he made a sign of caution and looked at Beth, she went on, "No use trying to keep it from her. He was outside here not half an hour ago—to meet Rose, I guess, because she showed up looking pale and frightened, and went away again with the lamest excuse I ever heard. But the thing is, the man mistook Beth for Rose and when she didn't answer the three-match signal he came after her to know what was up. If I hadn't had the door open when she got here, he'd have caught her. Ran just like a rabbit, she did."

Chris's face was white. "He didn't hurt you?"

At the expression in his eyes Beth's heart began to pound. "No, Chris, he never even caught up with me." She laughed. "Mummy is right. I should enter one of those hundred-yard-dash races. Bet I'd bring in a medal or whatever they get for winning them."

"Did you see his face? Would you know him again?"

She shook her head. "I just noticed that his hat was pulled down, covering his face. Anyhow, I was running too hard to stop for a look at him."

"Mummy is right," Chris said. "It's high time I began to escort you. From now on, young woman, I'm not going to let you out of my sight. Where you go I go until we put this fellow where he can't do any damage."

"Look here, Mummy, am I an individual or am I not?" The girl's mutinous eyes met Bradford's, though her words were for the old nurse. "Chris can hold back my allowance—and my husband. But he can't tell me whether I am to breathe or not. I am entitled to liberty and the pursuit of happiness."

She was very lovely as she proclaimed her own little declaration of independence. Under the black hat her hair showed glints of gold where the firelight caught it. Excitement had transmuted her eyes to deep, dark mysteries.

"That's mutiny," Chris declared. "It requires discipline." He caught his ward's hand and led her toward the door as he threatened her with mock severity. "Locked in your room and bread and water for a week, young woman."

Beth tucked her hand under his arm and smiled up radiantly into his face. "Pooh," she mocked. "I can wind you around my little finger."

A slow color mounted to Bradford's hair as he looked down at her and then glanced across at Martha Mumford.

Thank God, Chris is awake at last, the old woman thought, even as she said aloud with motherly impatience, "Run along now, children."

The air was crisp and tinglingly cool. There was a very young, slender moon traveling westward and the dark heavens looked as though they had been peppered with holes through which gleamed a golden lining. Beth gave a little sigh of utter content as the car moved swiftly along the road.

"Tired, Beth?" Chris asked tenderly.

"Tired? Of course not. I was enjoying this glorious air and having you all to myself. You are such a comfortable sort of person, Chris. I wonder if it's because you are not young and silly."

A tide of hot resentment swept over Bradford at her words. She had intimated once before that he was old. Did he seem staid to her? Had the cares which he had been obliged to assume so early stolen all semblance of youth from him?

He spoke abruptly. "Do I strike you as being a tyrant?" he asked, remembering his mother's word.

"Oh, I'm not complaining. I know my place and what a girl should expect from brothers."

"I am not your brother," Chris said quickly.

"There you go. Off with her head, again. Of course you are not my real brother, but you are my guardian, which is a heap sight worse," she added with spirit.

"There are advantages, though," he teased her. "I shall have something to say about the man you marry."

"Don't be so triumphant. You needn't worry about my marrying now."

"Why that emphasis on the *now*?"

"Nothing—only—"

"Only what?"

"What an autocrat you are, Chris! Well, then, if you will have it—when I heard Evelyn say she wouldn't marry you because of me, I planned to run away and get a job or—if worse come to worst—get married."

Chris looked down at the girl. She was nestled near him, her soft hair brushing his shoulder. Suddenly it seemed as though he must catch her in his arms, hold her close, press his lips to hers. The impulse was mad, savage, primitive. For a moment it overwhelmed him. He gripped the wheel with such force that the car swerved sharply to one side before he could steady it. What had happened to him? Was he in love with Beth? Had he loved her all the time? Good Lord, what a dolt he had been, what a blind fool.

Beth looked up with a lazy little laugh.

"What happened, Chris?"

"Nothing, except that I have just awakened to the fact that I may have missed the chance to get something I want very much."

"Don't do it again or you will have us in the ditch. What a heavenly night. I could ride on forever."

"Let's do it," he said recklessly.

"We have time to take the drive over the hill—but forever?" As he turned the car in response to her suggestion, she said, "What would become of all the widows and orphans in this town if you disappeared forever? The telephone wires would sizzle with frustrated cries of, 'Where's Chris?' No, there will never be any running away for you. You mean too much in this community!"

"Do you mind, Beth?"

"Mind? I'm so proud that my self-esteem visibly swells every time anyone says anything nice about you. Of course, part of that is personal pride. After all, I helped to bring you up. It's looking after me that has given you the strength of character and discipline that—"

"That have aged me so much?"

"Chris, how can you be so absurd?"

He was ridiculously pleased by her impatient comment. "Anyhow," he teased her, "you seem to like older men. What about Craven?"

"He isn't exactly bored when we meet," she drawled.

"The sophisticated type, that's you," Chris offered his cigarette case. "If you've become so worldly, how about a smoke?"

"You know I don't like that," she said, brushing the case away impatiently. "And I don't like Mark Craven simply because he is sophisticated. After all, he likes me." She rested her head against the back of the seat and tucked her hand confidentially under his arm.

Bradford's pulses gave a bound which maddened

him. He shook off her hand. "Don't touch my arm when I am driving!" he said sharply, and was sorry the moment the words left his lips. He felt her shrink away from him and sensed her look of hurt surprise. She sat very straight and still.

After a moment he said, "I'm sorry, Beth."

"I don't blame you," she answered quietly. "I can't possibly blame you for disliking me after the way I caused Evelyn to break the engagement."

"That's nonsense," he told her. "That wasn't because of you."

There was a moment's silence and then she inquired, "Chris, you know I couldn't help overhearing that conversation. What did she mean—about keeping me here so you could have the formula?"

The pause that followed puzzled her. Then Chris said, "Let's not talk about it now, Beth."

"As you like," she said coolly, and withdrew as far from him as the seat would allow.

"Beth—" he began impulsively.

"Evelyn is coming to dinner tonight," she told him.

"Evelyn!"

"She telephoned this morning and asked Nan. She is bringing Mr. Craven with her."

"So that's it," Chris exclaimed. "So that's it."

"Must you be so mysterious?"

He laughed. "All in all, it looks like an interesting evening. How does a rejected suitor behave, Beth?" When she made no reply, he suggested, "It might throw off some of those curious calculations people are bound to have about Evelyn and me if you and I were to appear interested in each other."

"You and I!" Beth exclaimed.

"Why not?"

"Interested in a child?" she mocked him. Then, suddenly, she repeated his words, "Why not?" He could not see the mischievous smile that touched the corners of her mouth, for she had turned her head away. "We'll do it," she said.

He laughed joyously. "Good. And as they say on the radio, 'We'll stump the experts.'"

As Beth and Chris walked back to the house from the garage Ted came to meet them.

"You're terribly late; you'll have to rush if you are going to dress. Everyone is here. Chris, the Duchess has come and she brought Mark Craven with her."

"Beth told me they were coming."

"Mother was sweet but icy when Evelyn suggested it. How the Duchess could have accepted that cold-storage consent I can't imagine." The boy's eyes were wide with anxiety. "Don't let her rope you in again, Chris."

"Don't worry. Anyone else here?"

"Just the Wednesday night regulars: Colonel Jim and Aunt Julia. Mother asked Smithy but he refused."

"Where is Smith tonight?" asked Bradford alertly.

"He had another engagement. I didn't know he had any acquaintances around here. He sticks to the house like a leech. I never knew such a conscientious guy. Hey, you two had better rush. Go in the back way."

Beth dashed for her room, bathed quickly, and started to dress. She reached for a brown taffeta dress, then after a moment's consideration put it back on its hanger and looked over her clothes. She took out a leaf-green velvet dress, with long sleeves and a deep V at the neck, which she had bought in Paris, and slipped it over her head. It fell to her feet in grace-ful folds. She brushed her curls, tight from her bath, into soft waves high on her head, fastened a string of pearls around her neck and smiled at the girl in the mirror.

If she was to help Chris and prevent him giving the appearance of being jilted, or—even worse—of be-ing available for recapture, she would have to be a credit to him. Chris. How odd he was lately. His peremptory manner. His sudden irritability in the car because she had tucked her hand under his arm, a gesture she had performed countless times before.

She stood before the mirror, no longer seeing her-self; seeing instead a new Chris, a Chris who was an older brother, a stranger with steady gray eyes and dark hair and finely cut lips. Not a stranger exactly, just an unknown quantity, but a disturbing unknown who could make her heart beat unsteadily.

When she came downstairs she entered the drawing room slowly, aware of the eyes that observed her.

Anne Bradford in a white gown was seated before the fire. Jim Haswell leaned against the mantel looking down on her. Beth wondered how she could sit there so calmly under his intent regard. If Chris had looked at her like that—Beth stood stock-still, her lips parted, her eyes wide with shock. So that was it! She no longer regarded Chris as a brother. He mattered to her more than anything in the world.

So this is the way love happens, she thought dazedly. Without warning. You walk in a room and everything is changed. She did not want to talk to people, she wanted to go away by herself, to consider this new knowledge of hers. But Chris was counting on her, counting on her help with Evelyn, and Chris must not be hurt.

"For heaven's sake, Beth," Julia Seagreave exclaimed, "you act like a somnambulist."

Julia, dressed in a glittering, steel-blue gown extravagantly décolleté, had adopted a romantic pose on the couch.

Craven, immaculate in dinner clothes, broke off his conversation with Evelyn, unusually lovely in a strapless yellow chiffon evening dress, to say, "Miss Gilbert is more like the sleeping beauty."

"Who is a sleeping beauty?" Chris demanded from the doorway.

Beth was not yet ready to meet his eyes. She was intensely aware of him, aware of Evelyn, aware of Julia's malicious eyes when they turned from Chris to Evelyn.

"Your ward," Craven said. He smiled down at Beth. "What awakened the sleeping beauty? As I remember the fairy tale, it was a kiss."

Beth was annoyed to feel herself blushing. It added to her confusion to realize, from the triumphant glint in his colorless eyes, that Craven believed he had brought the blush to her cheek.

Chris, too, saw her vivid coloring and Craven's avid and faintly amused eyes. He slid his hand under Beth's arm with an air of proprietorship. She raised her eyes to see him looking down at her, his own eyes glowing. It was only part of the game, of course, she reminded herself, but she returned the look with a tremulous smile. She was dimly aware of the startled expression on Nan's face, of the way Craven's eyes narrowed, of the way Evelyn's mouth hung half open in incredulous surprise.

To her relief, the dinner went off far better than she had expected. Anne Bradford was never more charming and winsome than when at the head of her own table. There was nothing artificial or stereotyped about her. She had an originality of thought and expression which kept her guests on the *qui vive*.

Tonight, she had to make little effort to keep the conversational ball rolling—all her family and guests seemed to be exerting themselves to be at their best. Craven devoted himself to Beth with an assiduity that whitened Evelyn's lips. Something in the naked hostility in her eyes when she looked at Beth made Chris strengthen his resolution to guard Beth every moment. If Evelyn ever had an opportunity to hurt his ward, she would not hesitate to do so.

Meanwhile, Beth was playing the game loyally, exchanging glances and laughing comments with Chris whenever the demands of her dinner partners made it possible for her to do so.

Craven was far too astute a man of the world to ignore his hostess for the sake of any woman, however alluring she might be—and Beth in her Parisian gown was more breathtakingly beautiful than he had realized. Whenever he turned to Mrs. Bradford, therefore—she had seated him on her right because he was the only stranger among her guests—he proved to be entertaining, amusing, with an unexpected fund of knowledge, keen observation from long and wide travel, and an innate awareness of her vulnerable weakness, her sons and her home.

Indeed, he talked so well that Colonel Haswell, on

her left, looked at her sharply and then relapsed into taciturn silence. Chris suppressed a smile because the colonel looked so like a big sulky boy.

As the evening wore on, Evelyn, who had devoted herself in the beginning exclusively to Mark Craven, turned to Chris in desperation. With cold politeness, Craven was making it brutally clear that if he had ever been interested in Evelyn Furnas that interest was now ancient history. He was openly paying attention to Beth, who, smiling and gay, and completely without coquetry, evaded him and drifted toward Chris. Not only Evelyn but Julia Seagreave observed their apparent absorption in each other. Craven's inexpressive face revealed nothing of his thoughts.

After dinner, the men drifted out onto the terrace to give advice on a plan Chris had been sketching for a new circular rose bed. While they stood arguing about location, the position of paths, various types of roses, grafting and spraying, Craven stood a little apart, leaning on a balustrade, twisting a small piece of paper between his fingers.

He was, Chris admitted to himself, an impressive-looking man. Evelyn and Julia were both obviously deeply interested in him. Would a girl as young as Beth be able to withstand the attentions of such a man? And why, after all, should she? Craven would be a fine match for any woman.

Chris turned as Rose came out with the coffee tray. While Colonel Jim was taking his cup, Chris saw Craven select a cigarette from a silver case and strike three matches while he attempted to light it. He was about to offer a lighter when he thought, Three matches!

Craven! Craven and Rose? Craven who had chased Beth that afternoon? Craven lurking in the orchard for a furtive meeting with a housemaid? He tried to remember the voice that had answered Rose's call. The voice that had said, "I told you not to telephone unless it was necessary. I don't like risks." Craven's? He could not be sure.

Rose had gone on to Ted, and now she brought the

tray to Chris. With a surprised gesture he motioned toward Craven. She hesitated and then took the tray to him.

Chris saw his guest fuss a little with the sugar tongs, then with a laughing apology help himself with his fingers. When he dropped the tongs something dropped with them onto the tray. A thin wad of paper.

When Rose came to him, Chris took his coffee, then picked up the crumpled bit of paper and tossed it idly over the wall of the terrace. The maid's face lost its color as he calmly helped himself to sugar.

Craven sipped his coffee, leaning against the wall of the terrace. A few dead leaves, still clinging tenaciously to the trees, rustled like a whisper of rain and hung motionless again—the air sharp with a hint of frost.

"What peace," Craven said. "I have never been a man for peace; the struggle for achievement stimulates me and gets in my blood. But there is something about the Manor—a serenity—I wonder, after all, if I am not missing something." Then he laughed, shaking off his mood. "Actually, I would die of dry rot and despair if I were not doing something."

"Doing what?" Chris asked.

"Making money," Craven said. "Building a fortune, feeling the challenge of outwitting the other fellow. That's the only real life, after all."

"Not mine," Chris admitted.

"So I gathered. That's why it surprises me that you are willing to give up all this in order to enter the hurly-burly and go into manufacturing. I understand you have the fabulous Gilbert formula."

"Fabulous," Chris replied noncommittally. "Well, that remains to be seen."

"I suppose," Craven said casually, "you've investigated—that you are sure it's the real thing."

"What do you mean—the real thing?" Chris was curious.

"Oh." Craven hesitated. "That it is all Gilbert claimed for it."

"I hope it is," Haswell broke in. Chris thought he

detected a strain of unholy joy in his voice. "It would knock the bottom out of the market for some of our present plastics."

Chris smothered a grin. So that was why Haswell had been writing so assiduously to his brokers. He was checking up on the stocks owned by Craven. Jealousy worked in peculiar ways.

"It can't be done," Craven said smoothly. "An inexperienced man, without vast capital and backing, simply cannot plunge into a new field and not lose his shirt. It has been tried over and over."

"Chris has a way of accomplishing what he sets out to do," Haswell murmured. "Ever hear of his war record?"

"That's the past," Chris intervened quickly. "Mother will feel we have deserted her."

He stood back to let his guests pass him. When they had gone he put his hands on top of the balustrade, vaulted lightly over onto the lawn and with a pencil flashlight searched for the paper. He smoothed it out.

"West gate at twelve," it read.

He hesitated for a moment, then crumpled it up and dropped it where he had found it, scrambled back on the terrace and went toward the house. As he reached the door, he saw Rose coming around the side of the house. He watched her search for the paper and slip it into her pocket.

VIII

The clock struck eleven as the guests departed. Evelyn hesitated for a moment and then said, "Mark, darling, I didn't see your car outside. Do let me give you a lift to the inn."

Chris stiffened, listening alertly. How, he wondered, would Craven avoid driving with Evelyn so that he could keep his twelve o'clock appointment at the west gate.

"Thanks so much," Craven said, "but I have a beastly headache and I'll get no sleep at all tonight unless I take a long walk." His voice was courteous but his eyes were implacable. Evelyn had the look of a person who has been ill as she turned away.

Only Colonel Jim and Julia Seagreave lingered. Ted escorted Julia to her car and when he returned he sank into a chair with a virtuous air. "Well," he declared to the world at large, "I think I deserve a medal. All evening I have exhausted myself entertaining Aunt Julia—by the way, she prefers to be called Julia. That word 'aunt' makes her sound too old, she tells me." He winked at Beth. "I never expected to see you try to rival Julia by taking all the men. The way you kept Chris and Craven eating out of your hand—"

"Think nothing of it," Beth said with an airy gesture. "It's just my natural charm."

"Well, *femme fatale*, before you get in your deadly work on me, I'm going to catch up on some sleep or Smithy will be disapproving tomorrow." Ted waved his hand and bounded up the steps two at a time.

Ignoring their banter, Colonel Jim took Anne Bradford's hand. "You look tired," he growled, glowering down upon her. "You do too much."

"Nonsense, Jim." She was her flushed, radiant self again. "I just took the evening too seriously. Between Mr. Craven and Evelyn I was afraid that it would be unpleasant." She walked toward the stairs, her hand still in Haswell's.

Alone in the drawing room with Chris, Beth turned slowly toward him, her heart thumping, conscious of her new knowledge about her feeling for him.

"Well, Chris," she said, trying to speak lightly, "I think we did very well."

He caught her hand with masterful possession and drew her toward him.

"You are beautiful in that leaf-green velvet dress," he said. "I could hardly take my eyes off you."

She looked at him in quick surprise. "You don't need to keep it up now they've gone," she reminded him.

His hands tightened on hers, his eyes glowing, his voice unsteady. "Perhaps I need practice," he said, his tone as light as hers but with something infinitely disturbing behind it. "How's this? I love you in that dress."

"You almost make me think you mean it. You get better and better."

She drew her hands away from his as they moved into the hall. "Good night, Colonel Jim," she said as the colonel turned away from the stairs and Anne Bradford slowly mounted them. Beth followed; half-way up she turned. Chris was still watching her. With a mischievous glance she blew him a little kiss and ran lightly on.

When the door of her room had shut behind her, Beth went to the window and curled up on the big window seat in the dark, looking out at the night, alone at last with her new knowledge.

Chris had always been important to her, always dear to her. But now he was everything. How, she wondered, could she keep him from suspecting how she felt about him? She remembered the impatient way he had brushed aside Evelyn's suggestion that he was interested in his ward. "Just a kid," he had said.

To him she was a ward, a responsibility, a kid to be looked after until she married.

This was a dangerous game she was playing, Beth confessed to herself, pretending to Evelyn that they were in love. Suppose Chris discovered that she was not playing? Suppose she was to be misled by some word or gesture of his, as she had almost been misled a few moments earlier, when he had so nearly drawn her into his arms? Suppose she had gone into his arms then, as she had longed to do, and rested her head against his shoulder, and lifted her lips to his. Her face burned with embarrassment in the dark.

Chris was gentle and infinitely kind. Suppose—suppose he should be sorry for her?

Hot tears stung her eyelids but she blinked them away. I owe Chris a tremendous lot, she reminded herself. I'll never make him sorry for me, never let him feel that he owes me anything. But I'd better—better go away soon.

She tried to imagine what it would be like to form a new life without Chris: Chris and his sound advice, his gay companionship, the tenderness in his voice when he spoke to her—except recently when he had been unexpectedly sharp. She remembered his annoyance when she had tucked her hand under his arm.

It would take a great deal of courage to leave the Manor. More courage, it seemed to her, than she had. She had been frightened in Europe when her room was searched over and over, when she had had that uncomfortable feeling, a sort of crawling along her spine, that she was being followed. Why had it happened? Suppose that were to happen again? At least, there had been no recurrence since her first night home.

A twig snapped under her window and she leaned out. Perhaps Chris couldn't sleep either. Perhaps he was walking in the garden. Someone was there but it wasn't Chris. Chris walked with a long free stride, his head up, his shoulders back. This man lurked. There was no other word for it. And his shoulders—they were exceptionally thick and massive. For a moment she was aware of a feeling of recognition. She had seen those heavy shoulders before. Then the man moved quickly and vanished into the darkness.

Somewhere there were muffled voices, quickly broken off. Then the west gate creaked. Something white drifted through it as noiselessly as fog, like— like a ghost.

Beth shivered with excitement and tension. Then the white figure gave a startled cry; for a moment Rose's face was caught in the beam of a flashlight and the maid was running wildly toward the house.

As Beth leaned to blow him a kiss from the stairs, Chris took a step after her and then checked himself. To his ward this was all a game. He was only Chris, old Chris, sober Chris, tyrranical Chris. The kiss was the curtain to the evening's act.

He turned to Haswell. "Come out on the terrace for a smoke before you leave, Colonel."

The older man gave him a keen glance. "Anything new?"

"I think so, yes."

For a few moments the two men paced up and down the terrace while Chris thought about Beth. Where Haswell's thoughts had drifted was obvious when he blurted out, "Who the devil is this man Craven?"

"Apparently you know more about him than I do by now," Chris said.

"I've been checking," the colonel admitted unabashed. "I wanted to know about a man whom your mother seems to find so immensely entertaining."

Chris stared in frank amazement. "He's not in love with Mother, Colonel Jim; it's Beth he's after."

"Oh," the colonel said rather blankly. "Anyhow, I've discovered that he is all that is claimed for him. He has built a solid fortune, and his investments are all sound. For three or four years he has been plunging heavily in plastics but they seem to be paying off. No one seems to know anything about him earlier than four years ago; he appeared out of the blue."

In a low tone Chris told him about Beth's experience with the man in the orchard, about Rose's appearance at Martha Mumford's, about the three matches which had attracted Chris's attention to the twisted note which had been intended for Rose and which she had later picked up.

"Craven!" the colonel exclaimed in surprise. "Then we have been on the wrong track all the time."

"I'm not sure," Chris said. "Craven said an odd thing tonight." He repeated Craven's comment about the formula.

"I see." The colonel dropped his cigar into a jardiniere. "What do you intend to do?"

"I think," Chris said, "it would be a sound idea if you and I were to be at the west gate at twelve."

"A very sound idea," the colonel agreed eagerly. "We may flush some game."

"It's about time," Chris told him. "Though if there is one thing I am sure of, it is that Craven is not our man. Hang it all, he was here all the time Beth was in Europe. He could not have followed her. And yet—she is in real danger. I feel that in my bones."

"There," Colonel Jim said firmly, "I fail to agree with you. I believe now as I did when you first discussed the matter with me that no one in his right mind would believe Gilbert would endanger his only child by entrusting the formula to her."

"Then why did someone—mad or sane—follow her through Europe, and search her room here the night she returned? And that could not have been Craven."

"Which brings it back to our original suspicions," Colonel Jim remarked cryptically.

As they continued their stroll up and down the terrace he added awkwardly, "So Beth is the object of Craven's assiduous attentions, not your mother."

Chris grinned in the darkness. "In any case," he said, "Craven is not the type of man to interest Mother."

"Who is?" Haswell said despairingly. "I suppose you know that I love her and always have. There were times after she married your father when I honestly tried to become interested in other women but somehow I couldn't make a go of it. As soon as I left them they faded like an old daguerreotype; I could see only Anne's face, hear only Anne's voice."

Chris laid his hand affectionately on the older man's shoulder. "Why don't you tell her that?"

"Do you mean it? How would you and Ted feel if she were to marry again? She would never willingly do anything to hurt either of you."

"We want Mother to be happy," Chris said, "and I know of no one who could come nearer than you to ensuring it, Colonel Jim."

"I can't tell you how I appreciate—" Haswell's fingers tightened about Chris's arm. "The fireworks are starting," he said in a low tone. "Something just moved over there under the trees. No—don't turn around. It's a man; two men, by Jove!"

Chris's low tone did not conceal his excitement. "Two! Then we were right, after all."

"I'm not sure. Neither of them is as tall as Craven. Are you sure you can handle this, Chris? It begins to look as though you are up against a strong combination."

"I'll handle it," Chris told him grimly.

It was a glorious night. The stars shone with unblinking clearness. The moon had scurried to the other side of the world hours ago.

"We can be seen here," Haswell reminded him softly. "The lights from the drawing room are streaming out on us."

Chris took his arm. "Good night, Colonel," he said clearly, and stood back to let the other man precede him into the house. He switched out the lights and they stepped onto the front porch and darkness. They waited a moment until their eyes became adjusted and then crept noiselessly off the porch, Haswell turning to the left and Chris to the right.

When the latter reached a spot from which he could observe the west gate he leaned back, sheltered by a thick hedge, and waited.

The night grew oppressively quiet. There was not

a breath of wind astir. From the village floated twelve measured strokes of a bell. Midnight. The reverberation died away in the distance. The silence became weird. Bradford waited impatiently. What had become of the two men in the shrubbery? Where was Craven?

What was that? Chris could see something moving above the top of the hedge on the street side. He shrank deeper into the shadow as a figure in white floated like mist toward the west gate. The hinge creaked as the gate was pressed open.

Chris leaned forward. Then, from somewhere on his left, a flashlight shone on the face of the figure standing at the open gate. It was Rose. The girl gave a low startled cry and fled toward the house. The flashlight switched off again. There was a low murmur of voices but no attempt to follow as the girl fled back to the house as though pursued by furies.

Now what, Chris wondered in bewilderment, was the object of that maneuver? If Craven wanted to meet the girl secretly he would never have thrown the flashlight beam on her face. Certainly, he would not have scared her away. Who then? Someone moved at his left and Chris turned swiftly in that direction, following the sound.

His foot kicked at a small pebble with a sound that was like thunder in the quiet night. The person on his left was moving fast now. And then he heard someone on his right, someone moving noisily, making no attempt to be silent. A match flared. John Smith, Ted's tutor, was lighting a cigarette and leaning casually against the gate.

"Good evening, Mr. Bradford," he said coolly, as he recognized Chris. "Are you enjoying the night air too?"

In the distance Chris heard the motor of a car turn over. The other man had got away. The tutor smiled faintly.

"A productive white spine variety of average size, six to eight inches in length, with broad and showy yellow and green foliage, habit of growth rampant—"

"Sounds like a coat of arms," Ted commented from his perch on the corner of the great desk in his brother's study.

"Don't interrupt," Beth said severely. "This list must be ready before I go to town tomorrow."

Ted shook his head in wonder. "Chris taking off two days just for fun, and driving you and Mother to New York. I don't get it. Lately he's been so busy he hardly has time for meals and then all of a sudden he decides to have a holiday. It must be love." He looked up suddenly. "I hope that's it," he said soberly. "It would be swell if you and Chris—lately I've thought—"

Beth felt the color burning her skin. "Nonsense," she said crisply. "Chris and I are just playing a game to discourage Evelyn in case she should get any ideas."

Ted studied her for a moment in silence. "Now who had that idea, I wonder."

"Chris."

"To discourage Evelyn?" he scoffed. "Chris doesn't need any help of that kind. I'll bet it was to discourage Craven."

Beth laughed. "Whatever the reason, we've got to get these seeds ordered and, as I took it on myself to superintend the planting of the kitchen garden, it's up to me to be on time even if I have to depend on last year's catalog. Where was I? Oh, yes. Growth rampant, fruit long and slim, dark green throughout the entire length with a slight white marking at the blossom end. That's what we want. Put down one ounce Improved White Spine."

"Whose white spine?" Ted demanded.

"Cucumber, of course."

Ted sighed. "You look so glamorous and you're just a farmer at heart. Other girls may yearn for orchids or swoon over gardenias. It takes you to get sentimental over squashes like corpulent footballs, tomatoes gay with red paint." His words died away as he saw that the girl's attention had drifted off, that she was dreaming, her eyes under her long extravagant lashes wandering around the room.

Chris's room, Beth thought. Everything in the place was stamped with his interests and his personality. Along the wall hung his diplomas and the photographs of the teams on which he had played in college. Below them was a cabinet filled with cups he had won and baseballs he had pitched in winning games. In one corner a safe had been built in. On either side of the great fireplace tier upon tier of books rose to the ceiling. There were filing cabinets and deep easy chairs.

There were two photographs on the desk, a fine one of Anne Bradford, and a hand-colored one of Beth, taken at the age of fourteen, the one over which Evelyn had laughed, calling her a freak.

Ted chuckled. "When you have finished admiring your own loveliness we will proceed with the business of the afternoon."

Beth picked up the catalogue and then called, "Come in," as someone knocked on the door. Ted twisted around on his perch to inspect the intruder.

It was Rose, pale, with red-rimmed eyes. "Miss Furnas is here," she said in a low tone, "and Mrs. Bradford would like you to join them for tea."

"I'll come at once," Beth promised. When the maid had gone she implored, "Come with me, Ted."

"Listen to the Duchess when I don't have to? Nothing doing. Evelyn has her claws out for you and as long as Mother won't let me spit and scratch in your defense I'd better keep away."

He was out of the Dutch door before Beth could protest. She got reluctantly to her feet. In the past week Mark Craven had called her almost daily, asking her to lunch (sorry, but she was busy) to dinner (she had another engagement) to cocktails (she didn't drink). During the same time Evelyn had called him almost an equal number of times at the inn (information relayed country-fashion by the desk clerk to the head waiter to the Bradford cook, who was his cousin, and by her to Beth). And now she was making another attempt to recapture Chris.

Reluctantly, Beth collected her catalogues and papers and placed them in a cabinet. She straightened the blotter on top of the desk, postponing as long as possible her meeting with Chris's ex-fiancée. As she turned the blotter her eyes were caught by her own name—Elizabeth Gilbert—in reverse in Chris's handwriting. She bent over it. A girl in love was absurd, she told herself, when she could get such rapture out of seeing her name written by the man she loved. Elizabeth Gilbert. Why had Chris been writing her name? There were other words on the blotter, which had been used only once. Elizabeth Gilbert—and then, not easy to make out, because they appeared backwards, a few other words appeared. In her mind she turned the letters around: . . . *guarded* . . . *wrong formula* . . . *Sergent* . . . *killed* . . . What on earth did it mean? That her father's trusted assistant, Larry Sergent, had been killed and that her father's formula was "wrong," worthless? That all his efforts and sacrifice had been for nothing? Why hadn't Chris told her?

She remembered that she was expected in the drawing room. She squared her shoulders, took a deep breath, and left the study. Mrs. Bradford was reading a note when she entered. Near the tea wagon, her costly furs thrown back, her light hair almost golden in contrast with the dark fur of her toque, Evelyn Furnas was sitting. The firelight transformed the jewels on her black dress into a myriad little glimmering rainbows. Her eyes were cold and hard and china-blue as she looked at the girl who entered.

"Beth," Anne said, "Colonel Jim has just been made a present of some choice game and he wants us to dine with him tonight. Shall I accept for you?"

"Of course."

Beth poured herself a cup of tea while Mrs. Bradford excused herself to leave the room and answer the note, busied herself with sugar and cream, and finally looked across at Evelyn. On the latter's left hand she saw the circlet of diamonds which Chris had given her and a little spasm of terror gripped her heart. Could this cold, inexorable girl hold the man whom she had discarded?

Evelyn's eyes followed hers and she smiled faintly.

"Beth," she said, "you can't have Chris. Is that clear to you?"

"What on earth—?"

"You know what I mean," Evelyn said impatiently. She glanced toward the door to make sure that they were alone. "I was engaged to Chris and I intend to marry him."

"But you broke your engagement."

"A lover's quarrel," Evelyn said lightly. "I saw the way Chris looked at you at the dinner party, as though you were Helen of Troy and the Venus de Milo and Cleopatra all rolled into one. It didn't impress me much. That's why I thought you and I had better have a little talk, so you would know where you stand."

Beth got to her feet. "I'm not interested, Evelyn," she said steadily.

Evelyn's eyes narrowed. "Oh, yes, you're interested. You think I'm your enemy, Beth, but actually I am your friend. I hate seeing you made a fool of. You think Mark Craven has fallen in love with you and that Chris is under your thumb. Well, they aren't. There's only one thing about you that interests them—and that is the Gilbert formula. If you didn't have that, neither one of them would give you a second thought. You might as well get that straight."

"I don't believe you," Beth said steadily.

Evelyn laughed. "Why do you think Mark Craven wanted me to bring him here? Because he was swept off his feet by you? That's childish. He wanted to find out about your father's formula. *He told me so.* I'm not guessing. As for Chris—" She shrugged her shoulders. "Chris is no fool. He knows where the formula is now. And he's the only man who does. And he wants to make sure he can hang on to it."

"And you would be willing to marry a man if you thought that about him?" Beth said in wonder.

"I am going to marry Chris. So—I warn you, Beth. *Keep out of my way.*"

She broke off and lighted a cigarette as Anne came back into the room.

"Where's Chris?" she asked Anne with a challenging look at Beth.

"I'm afraid you can't see him this afternoon, Evelyn. He is up to his chin in work." In her eagerness to make clear that Chris was not available, Mrs. Bradford rushed on. "He is clearing up things so he can drive us to New York tomorrow."

"How perfect," Evelyn exclaimed. "I am going in to Maizie Towle's debut and I've been dreading the train. Tell Chris to give me a ring so I'll be ready when he comes to pick me up."

Beth looked imploringly at Mrs. Bradford.

"Sorry, Evelyn," the latter said crisply, "but I'm afraid we can't do that."

Evelyn looked at her in startled incredulity. Then her face whitened with anger. "Do you mean that you refuse to take me?"

"I'm afraid," Anne said gently, "that is exactly what I mean."

Evelyn rose and drew her furs about her throat. "Well," she said, "now we know where we stand." She went out of the room without a backward glance.

"Anne," Beth said unsteadily, "I am afraid you have made an enemy."

Anne Bradford smiled at her reassuringly. "Don't look so upset, my dear." The smile deepened. "What a pity Ted wasn't here. He said I was wax in people's hands." She laughed outright but there was no answering laughter in Beth's troubled eyes.

IX

Just as they were about to leave the house for dinner at Colonel Haswell's, the telephone rang.

Anne Bradford sighed in resignation. "Someone is in trouble again and wants Chris," she said.

But Rose, who had answered the telephone, turned around. "It's for you, Miss Gilbert. Mr. Craven is calling."

"Miss Gilbert?" Craven's voice said eagerly. "It's such a wonderful night. I hope you'll come for a ride with me after dinner. I'll pick—".

"What a pity," Beth exclaimed. "We are just leaving the house to dine with Colonel Haswell. Perhaps you'll let me go another time."

Craven laughed confidently. "There will certainly be another time, Miss Gilbert. Many of them, in fact. I think fate intends us to see a great deal of each other from now on."

While Ted went out to get the car. Chris's eyes signaled Beth and she followed him into his study.

"What did Craven want?" he asked crisply.

"He asked me to go for a ride tonight. I said no. But you heard that."

"You also suggested you might give a different answer some other time. Let's have it clear once and for all. I forbid it."

"Really, Chris," the girl flared. "There are times when you go too far."

"I have a reason," he said. "Anyhow"—the stern look faded and he smiled at her—"Mother tells me that Evelyn was wearing my ring again when she came for tea this afternoon. If we are to make our story convincing, it won't help if you go out with Craven, will it?"

"You keep saying that you have a reason, Chris, but what is your reason?" Beth demanded, tilting back her head so that her eyes met his levelly.

He shook his head. "Not yet," he said.

"Now," she insisted. "I won't be ordered around without knowing the reason. And I won't go on pretending that—that"—her voice broke for a moment and then became crisp—"that we are in love with each other."

"And I thought we were doing so well," he said with mock disappointment. "Perhaps you aren't really trying." His hands were on her shoulders and he was looking down at her intently. "You should go to more movies like Mummy," he said laughing. Unexpectedly he bent over her and brushed her lips lightly with his own. Then his hands dropped and he stepped back quickly. "We'd better go," he said brusquely.

"Don't do that again, Chris," Beth said so sharply that he was startled. "Never do that again." She hastened past him, pulling her coat over her shoulders, hoping that he would not notice how she was trembling.

Nan was already seated in the front of the car with Ted at the wheel. Chris helped Beth into the back seat and saw in surprise that she shrank into her own corner, huddled in her coat. He should not have risked the kiss, he admitted to himself, feeling about her as he did, but he had not dreamed that it would make her so angry.

In her own corner Beth was hearing Chris's words, "I have a reason." But what reason? And why was he so absurd about Mark Craven's attentions? The formula, Evelyn had said. "If you didn't have that, neither of them would give you a second thought."

The car stopped at Colonel Haswell's, brought up with a flourish by Ted, and Chris helped his mother out and then gave Beth his hand. His eyes met hers with anxious tenderness as she hesitated for a moment. Then she smiled her old radiant smile, put her hand in his, and jumped out lightly.

Colonel Jim's housekeeper led Nan and Beth into

a guest room where they could leave their wraps.

"This dinner was sort of short notice," she said apologetically. "But I do hope everything will be all right. The butler hasn't had a lot of experience but I know you will make allowances."

Nan smiled at the housekeeper. "Just as though you didn't know that the wheels in your domestic machinery couldn't wobble. You are the admiration and despair of every housekeeper in the county."

Mrs. Altman beamed with gratification. "It's like you to say that, Mrs. Bradford, but I am getting old now and the care of the house worries me. Servants aren't what they were once. I wish the colonel would marry but—" She checked herself with a slow flush, which was reflected in Anne Bradford's face. "If you have everything you want," she said hastily, and left the room.

Ted, having served his purpose as chauffeur, had returned home with laughing martyrdom, to prepare for the following day's work with his tutor. Beth, looking around the candlelit table, thought that this would be a delightful dinner if only she had not quarreled with the man who sat across from her and who seemed determined to meet her eyes across the mound of delicate green and white stevia between them. Nan was more glowing than Beth had ever known her to be. It would be difficult, Beth thought, for anyone to believe that a woman so gentle and radiant and delightful could be the one who, only a few hours earlier, had dealt with Evelyn in so incisive a manner. Where her sons were concerned Nan Bradford would fight like a tigress.

Colonel Jim had flung aside his taciturnity of the last dinner party, during which he had sat and glowered at Mark Craven. Tonight he was jovial, happy, devoting himself entirely to Nan. Had he made up his mind at last to win the woman he loved? Something in his determined air made Beth smile to herself. After all, that was the only way for any man to feel about the woman he loved, that she must marry him. Suppose Nan did marry the colonel?

Where would she live, here at his house or at the
Manor? But it was difficult to imagine the Manor
without Nan!

"Come back, Beth," Chris laughed, his voice and
his eyes compelling hers with an intentness, a warmth,
a determination that were like those in the colonel's.
As though, Beth thought, either Nan or Haswell
would notice anyone but themselves tonight. Chris
was playing his part well, almost alarmingly well.
"Come back," he repeated.

"I was nearer than you think," she said lightly, and
joined in the conversation.

While coffee was being served in the living room,
Craven was announced

"Sorry," he said as he shook hands with Haswell.
"I dropped in in search of conversation. I had no idea
you had guests."

His eyes sought Beth, informing her without words
that he had come in search, not of conversation, but
of her.

Conscious of Haswell's effort to be cordial, of
Chris's new sternness, which made him almost a
stranger, Beth attempted to lighten the atmosphere
by the warmth of her greeting. Then a glance from
Chris reminded her of her new role and she aban-
doned Craven to his fate while she devoted herself to
Chris. They sat with their heads together, talking confidentially. The effect on the others must be of their
having a thousand secrets to exchange. Beth wondered
what they would think if they knew she and Chris
were actually discussing the vegetables which she had
ordered for the kitchen garden. She stifled a giggle.

"Now you are here, Craven, we can have some
bridge," Haswell said. "Beth doesn't play."

Craven, who obviously had every intention of breaking up the twosome, was taken aback and ill pleased,
but his good manners came to his rescue and he settled down at the table with Nan, Chris and Haswell.

Beth curled up in a deep chair near the fire. The
reflection turned her white dress to rose and each
sparkling crystal on it became a point of light. For a

few moments she watched the four at the card table, seeing Nan expand in beauty like a flower coming to full bloom under the devotion in the colonel's eyes. That was what love could do to a woman when it settled deep in her heart. In spite of herself, Beth felt a twinge of envy when she compared Nan's growing happiness with the shadowy romance she and Chris were carrying on. She remembered the engagement ring gleaming defiantly on Evelyn's left hand, and the threat in Evelyn's voice.

That much was real, at any rate, the enmity of the girl who was determined to marry Chris although she had once jilted him and did not love him even now. She shan't trick him into marriage, Beth vowed to herself. It would ruin his life, and a woman as unscrupulous as Evelyn would descend to any stratagem to get him.

She set her lips firmly as she determined to play the game with Chris, but in spite of herself her eyes filled with tears. A shadowy romance was a cold thing, a lonely thing. She thought of the line in Tennyson's "Lady of Shalott": "I am half sick of shadows." She brushed the moisture from her eyes and watched the castles and caves in the red coals as they shifted and faded and flared.

She looked up as footsteps sounded on the polished floor. Stone had come into the room to remove the coffee tray. She looked at him absent-mindedly at first, then her attention was alerted. An elusive memory tantalized her. Something about the man was familiar. She studied the lined, impassive face, the sleek brown hair. What did he remind her of?

As he turned in the doorway, something in his walk jolted her memory. Those massive shoulders. Surely, that was the man who had been in the garden the night Rose had crept in like a ghost! No, she remembered seeing the gleam of a bald head and this man had brown hair. She must be letting her imagination get away from her again.

The butler had gone without a backward look, although he had lingered in the room as long as he possibly dared. Why? In the mirror over the fireplace she had seen his eyes move in sharp, darting glances over Chris to Craven to Haswell. If he hoped to overhear any conversation he was disappointed, for the table was silent except for the bids.

Beth straightened up in her chair. It was no coincidence that Rose at the Manor and the butler at Colonel Haswell's were given to eavesdropping. Something was desperately wrong. She suspected that Chris knew what it was and had no intention of telling her. Well, it was time she did something herself.

"High time," she murmured.

"What is it, Beth?" Chris was leaning over the back of her chair.

"Craven is playing this hand," he explained as she looked over his shoulder at the group he had left. "I've been watching you. Your face is like a mirror with the thoughts chasing each other over it. I watched you wonder in perplexity and then come to a big decision. A penny for them?"

She glanced up at him. He leaned nearer with a light in his eyes so intense, so demanding, that the girl instinctively raised her hand to keep him back.

The look changed. "What is it, Beth? Don't be angry with me. I don't think I could bear that." The tenderness, the emotion in his tone affected her like an irresistible magnet. The hand that had repelled him groped blindly toward him.

"Your deal, Bradford," Craven's voice cut in.

With a muttered word Chris turned away and Beth's hand dropped to her side. Did Chris think it necessary to carry on the pretended romance for Craven's benefit? The thought hurt unbearably.

She got swiftly to her feet and started across the room. She stopped to study a picture here, straighten a book there, until she reached the door. Once she was on the other side, it was a simple matter to locate the butler. She heard him moving in Colonel Jim's den at the end of the hall where the men always left their coats.

As she touched the door it swung lightly open. She

held her breath while she looked into the room. Stone was too preoccupied to notice her. Again she saw the massive shoulders, the line of his sleek brown hair. When she realized what he was doing she entered the room swiftly.

"Stone!" she exclaimed.

He turned like a startled animal and straightened up. "Yes, Miss Gilbert," he said expressionlessly.

"I'll have to report this to Colonel Haswell."

"I hope you won't do that, miss. It would mean losing my job. For a middle-aged man that's a tragedy."

Beth shook her head. "I'm sorry. The colonel is my friend. I can't keep quiet while you are in this house behaving like a spy."

The man studied her, his eyes seeming to note automatically—as indeed they did—the shape of her eyes, the color of her hair, each feature neatly docketed and put away in a mental file. At length he made up his mind.

"In a way," he said, "there's a certain element of truth in that." His tone was no longer the expressionless, trained one of Stone the butler. It was more succinct, more alert, less subservient. "But I can assure you that I am not spying on Colonel Haswell." Once again he estimated her. "I must rely on your honor to protect my secret, Miss Gilbert. A great deal hinges on it. A vast amount of harm can be done if my real position here should be exposed at this time."

"What is your real position?" Beth inquired.

He felt in his pocket, drew out a wallet which he opened and handed to her wordlessly. Under the cellophane film was a card reading: *Thomas E. Stone, Investigations.*

"You are a detective!" she exclaimed.

He glanced quickly at the door and then nodded his head.

"But who—"

"I can't tell you that now. But I must repeat that if you reveal who I am you may do a great wrong, a terrible wrong, one in which a human life is involved."

Some instinct in Beth believed him. "Well," she said uncertainly. Then she made up her mind. "All right, Stone, I won't say anything." She started to leave the room and then remembered what had first aroused her interest in him, the similarity between his shoulders and those of the bald man in the garden.

"Why were you in the garden at the Manor the other night?"

"In the garden at the Manor?" he repeated in bland surprise. "You must be mistaken."

Beth was perplexed. After all, she had seen the man as little more than a moving shadow with thick bunched shoulders and a gleaming bald head.

"Is Colonel Haswell in any danger?" she asked. "Will your being here cause him any trouble? I can't sit back and say nothing while the colonel—"

"You need not worry about the colonel," the butler-detective assured her. "And I repeat, Miss Gilbert, a human life is involved."

Beth studied him in an agony of indecision. At length she turned to leave the room. Suddenly Stone was between her and the door.

"I must have your word of honor, Miss Gilbert."

There was nothing to be read in his face. Beth waited for the space of a half dozen heart beats.

"I give you my word," she said steadily.

Stone stepped aside. "I can trust that," he said. "It is my business to know people. Good evening, Miss Gilbert."

Several hours earlier, Rose had stood at the door until the Bradfords and Beth Gilbert left for the dinner party at Colonel Haswell's. Everyone was gone now, except for Mr. Smith. She would not be missed if she left the house. But should she go? If she did, it would be for the last time, the very last time. She stood shivering beside the closed door, thin hands clenching and unclenching at her sides, clutching

desperately at the decision at which she had slowly
and painfully arrived during the past few days.

The pretty face was drawn and colorless and her
lips twitched while she put on her hat and coat. She
hurried out into the crisp November air. The sky
above her head was powdered with stars, a delicate
hoarfrost whitened the hedges and glistened on the
hard brown road.

How often she had walked down this dark road toward the village, and always, as now, with her heart
pounding in fear, her feet dragging reluctantly toward
the impending interview, feeling like a chained cap-
tive who could not free herself from her fetters.

He would be waiting for her in the orchard behind the waffle shop. As she passed the little building,
with its swinging sign, its brass doorknob gleaming,
its crisp curtains at the windows, she was reminded
of the afternoon when she had been driven there by
an intolerable need for help and advice, only to be
stopped by the sight of Elizabeth Gilbert. She could
not talk before a third person. So she had stammered
out a stupid excuse that neither of them had believed,
and had gone away.

Slowly she entered the dim lane that led to the orchard behind the waffle shop. For a moment she
looked around but there was no sound. The trees were
bare now. Summer and warmth had gone; it seemed
to her that they would never come again.

She seated herself on a boulder and waited, shivering, her coat pulled tight about her. For the last
time, she comforted herself. The last time. The town
clock boomed six. For a few moments after the last
stroke of the bell the air vibrated and then settled
into stillness. An adventurous cricket, which must
have read the month wrong on its calendar, piped
once, shrilly.

Then a man turned off the road onto the path.
Rose saw a tiny spark, then another and another. She
got up stiffly to meet the man who hurried toward
her.

"What happened the other night?" he demanded.

"Didn't you find my message after Bradford threw it over the terrace wall? That was a bad moment. I thought certainly he would look at it."

"Yes, I found it. I was at the west gate at twelve, Mark, but someone else was there, someone with a flashlight. It was turned full on my face and I was so startled I couldn't think of any excuse for being there so I just turned and ran."

Mark Craven lighted a cigarette and nodded thoughtfully. "There was someone around all right. I got there just a minute or so after twelve and I could hear talking. I got out in a hurry."

"You took an awful chance, dropping that note right in front of Mr. Chris."

"Mr. Chris." He laughed. "You've picked up the authentic tone of the loyal family servant. Rose, you are really a wonder. But you're right. It was a risk and we won't try that again."

"No," Rose said softly, "we won't try that again."

He did not notice her inflection. "Well, we haven't much time. I am going back to the inn for dinner and then I want to drop in at Colonel Haswell's afterwards. What have you found out?"

"I overheard a conversation between Mr. Chris—I mean Mr. Bradford," she corrected herself, "and Colonel Haswell. Mr. Bradford has the formula—"

Craven gave a low exclamation. "Sure of that?"

She nodded and then realized he could not see her in the dark. "Yes, I'm sure."

"Where is it?"

"In the safe in his study."

"Nonsense! He wouldn't be such a fool as to leave a thing that may be worth millions where any housebreaker could lay hands on it. Anyone can crack those home safes."

When she made no reply he turned her toward him sharply so that the dim street lamp would reveal her face. "Is that the truth?"

She looked at him with miserable, haggard eyes. "Would I dare tell you anything else?"

"What is the combination?"

She was silent for a long time. At length she said, "Mr. Chris—ah—Mr. Bradford keeps it in a small notebook that he locks in his desk."

"Get it for me."

"Mark," she wailed. "I can't. I won't."

His fingers tightened cruelly over her arm. She cringed without seeming to know how to protect herself.

"Why else did I send you to Bradford's house? I want that formula. I intend to have it." He added in a puzzled tone, "So Bradford had the right one all the time. Somehow I just sent you there on a hunch—thought you might pick up something from conversation or Bradford's mail. I never thought I'd hit the jackpot. I'd about come to the conclusion that Gilbert had given the thing to his daughter."

"Mark, are you the one who searched her room the night she got here?"

"What's that!"

She gave a low cry of pain. "You are hurting me." He dropped her arm.

"Now, what is all this about?"

She told him about the ransacking of Beth's room. "But nothing was missing," she declared.

"So—" For a moment Craven brooded. "Well, there's no time to lose. After all I have done, I don't intend to lose out now. We've got to hurry, that's all. Get me that combination to the safe, Rose. And I don't care how you get it."

"And suppose—suppose I refuse to do it?"

He laughed softly, caught her in his arms and crushed her lips under his, holding her until she ceased to struggle and leaned weakly against him. He laughed triumphantly down into her eyes.

"Do you refuse?" he mocked. "Do you?"

Her eyes blazed at him from her white face. She wrenched herself free. "Yes," she panted, "yes, I do."

Before he was aware of her intention she had turned and was running wildly down the orchard path toward the road. With an oath he took after her but he was too late. She had already reached the road and the lights of the village. He dared not pursue her there. His jaw set and his eyes smoldered while he watched her move farther and farther away from him, out of his reach.

X

Rose heard Craven's oath of anger before she started to run along the path. Once she caught her foot in a root and crashed to the ground. Almost stunned by the force of her fall, she struggled up and ran on. When she reached the lighted street she instinctively pulled her hat into place and walked slowly. Her breath still came in gasps. She tried to control it, stopping to look into shop windows, hoping that the slower pace would quiet her pounding heart. She looked furtively over her shoulder. Craven was not in sight. He would never venture to follow her where he might be seen and recognized.

Where had she found the courage to burst the shackles which held her? He had been surprised by her cry of defiance, of liberation, but no more than she herself had been. Somewhere she had acquired the strength to face the punishment which he would inevitably mete out. Thank God, she had found it. There could be no turning back now.

But before making her break for freedom she had, as a price of her own freedom, performed one more act of dishonor. She had told him that the formula was in the Bradford safe. True, she had not divulged the combination, which she had found carelessly lying in Christopher Bradford's unlocked desk drawer. But she had no illusion. Craven would be clever enough to open that safe in one way or another, even if he had to take the terrible risk of blowing it up.

She walked on slowly and was caught in a little crowd of people who were waiting to buy tickets for a movie. She allowed herself passively to be engulfed by it and swept along to the ticket window. Perhaps the picture would help her to forget her problems for a while. When her mind was rested she could decide what to do.

But her own thoughts dominated. Seated in the dark theater she stared unseeingly at the film. She lived over again her acquaintance with Craven. Her first position in New York had been that of cashier and stenographer in a brokerage office. The firm was not of the highest type—she had become aware of that shortly after she had started to work—but her funds were too low to admit of fastidiousness. Gradually, she had become callous to the business methods which in the beginning had shocked her.

Craven had seemed to be a sort of silent partner in the concern. Any business in which he was interested was always conducted behind closed doors; he never appeared in the open. Rose knew that he and the two other men had blown several get-rich-while-you-wait bubbles, which had been alluringly iridescent and unbelievably profitable while they floated. Of course, they had followed the law of bubbles and collapsed, but not until after the inflaters had wafted them into other hands.

The girl had been thrilled by the Aladdin-and-the-wonderful-lamp tales of fortunes piled up in one deal, of expensive cars purchased from the profits of one day's juggling. At length, thoroughly inoculated with the poison of her surroundings, she had flung her savings into the vortex of frenzied speculation. They were speedily sucked under, and to save them she "borrowed" from the cash drawer without asking the firm's permission. But her effort to save her little hoard was as futile as an attempt to arrest the ebbing tide.

Of course, her employers found her out. Equally of course, they discharged her without a reference, reminding her of their forbearance in not having her arrested. Mark Craven watched it all with his colorless eyes.

Rose went from place to place in search of work. Naturally she could find no job without references. Craven knew of her efforts and pretended to befriend her. He lent her money but he never used his influence to get her work. The man held a certain fascination for the girl, against which she fought desperately, but he was subtle and convincing and she was naturally frank and credulous. For a while she had drifted along in fancied security—and then had come a revelation which had stunned her.

When she emerged from the maze in which she had been caught, she looked for a position as a housemaid. She had tried long enough to get office work but no one would hire her. She discovered, however, that women were so eager to secure domestic help that they would engage servants without references. She worked tirelessly and honestly, and at the end of a year had become an expert parlormaid. Little by little she paid back the money she had taken from the office. During all that time she heard nothing from Craven, and she hoped passionately that he had passed out of her life forever.

One day she received a newspaper which contained a market advertisement for a maid to go to the country. She was hungry for the freedom and freshness of out of doors and eagerly answered it, assuming that an employment agency had suggested the opportunity. Mrs. Bradford had hired her and the girl had fallen in love with her at once. A month after her arrival at the Manor, her hardly acquired contentment and sense of security vanished as suddenly as a ray of sunlight before an onsweeping tempest. Craven had stopped her on the street.

He had explained that he had sent the paper containing the marked advertisement, that he had never lost sight of her, that she was to secure certain information from the Bradford household and pass it on to him. When Rose protested vehemently, he observed that either she would do as he said or he would inform Mrs. Bradford of the truth about her past.

Rose had felt as though a gigantic cuttlefish had seized her in its tentacles and was crushing her into submission. With a wild, frenzied desire to retain Mrs.

Bradford's respect, to keep her in ignorance of what she had done, the girl had consented to Craven's plan.

Now, on the big screen in the darkened theater, reel after reel of the movie unfolded before Rose's eyes, but its meaning did not penetrate her consciousness. The drama of her own life, which throbbed and flamed with shame and fear, made the people of the screen seem like drab, wooden marionettes. Her heart ached unbearably when she thought of the past. She had swerved from the path of honor and it seemed as though there was no possibility of getting back. She had been horribly to blame for it; she had been tempted and her will had weakened, then she had stopped fighting. She had no excuse to offer for herself. No human being can stop doing what she knows to be right just because it is hard, she thought sadly.

She shook herself mentally. She was losing courage again. She must not look back. She would go forward. Her face was drained of color and the hands gripped in her lap were rigid and clammy. No matter what came of it she would break Craven's hold.

As the lights went on in the theater, a voice said, "How did you like the picture, Rose?"

The voice brought her back to her surroundings with a start. A man was seated beside her. Her cold cheeks warmed as she saw the earnest face and kindly eyes behind the horn-rimmed spectacles. Mr. Ted's tutor, Mr. Smith, had taken the seat beside her in the darkness.

"I didn't see it, Mr. Smith," she admitted. "I've been puzzling over a problem." She expelled a long, shaking breath. "I can't decide what to do."

"Perhaps I can help," he suggested gently.

Rose was hesitant. She longed to talk to this man, whose kindliness warmed her, made her feel less lonely. But suppose the only result would be to disgust him, or worse, to make him report to Mrs. Bradford what he had learned about her past? She got up without answering and Mr. Smith followed her out through the lobby.

"Suppose," he suggested quietly, "we stroll for a little while before we go back to the Manor. Are you warmly enough dressed for that?"

"Oh, yes," Rose said eagerly, glad to postpone for a little longer her return to her room, with her problems still unsolved.

Side by side, they walked along the village street, out beyond the lights along a country road. It was very still. There was no sound at all but their footsteps. The tutor's hand slipped under her arm and she felt a sense of warmth, of protection, of wellbeing. He made no effort to prompt her, to hurry her into speech. Perhaps if he had done so she would not have spoken at all. It was his silence that encouraged her.

"Suppose," she said abruptly—"suppose you had done something bad—not because you meant to but because you—well—sort of *had* to. And you could make up for it, only you'd get yourself into a terrible mess. What would you do?"

He was thoughtful for a moment. Then he said, "I think I'd take a chance and try to straighten it up. But are you sure you'd get yourself into serious trouble?"

"Yes," she said shortly, "I am."

They walked on slowly. At last she said desperately, "I've got to talk about it or I'll go crazy."

"I want you to. Perhaps, as I said, I can help."

"No one can help me, but if I could just relieve my mind—You see, there's—someone—who wants that formula Mr. Chris has." The tutor's hand tightened spasmodically over her arm; for a moment he paused and then he walked on at her side.

"He—this person knows something—something about me that would make Mrs. Bradford dismiss me." Her voice broke. "And I could be so happy here, so safe, if I could only stay." She wiped her eyes and steadied her voice. "He—this person—had me find out where the formula is—"

"Quite a job," the tutor said dryly.

"No," the girl contradicted him. "It wasn't hard. I

listened at Mr. Chris's study hour and one day I heard him tell Colonel Haswell he had the formula in his safe. When I was cleaning the study I—well, I looked in his desk and there was the combination to the safe. So"—she caught back a sob—"tonight I told—this person—where the formula was."

"And gave him the combination to the safe?"

"No—I pretended I didn't have it. But it won't make any difference. He—this person is bound to get it."

There was a long silence. The tutor's tight grasp of her arm relaxed, his hand slid down and clasped her hand in his, in a gentle sort of way, and they walked on in silence hand in hand.

"We'll have to go back," Rose said at last. "It is getting late and I went out without permission."

"Yes," Smith agreed, "we'll have to go back. Poor little girl, you've had a lot on your mind, haven't you?"

His sympathy brought tears to her eyes.

"Let's see"—he seemed to be thinking aloud—"what we can do about it, so that we can rectify your mistake and still keep you out of it." He thought for a moment. "How's this?" he asked abruptly. "Suppose you give me the combination to the safe. I'll take out the formula so this—this person—can't get it. Then after—this person—has ransacked the safe—I'll put the formula back where Mr. Bradford will have it and you won't be guilty of anything at all. How does that strike you?"

"It's—it's wonderful," she said unsteadily. "But isn't that an awful risk for you to take? Suppose Mr. Chris catches you opening his safe?"

"He won't," Smith laughed confidently.

"But why," she asked, "would you take such a risk for me?"

"Someday I'd like to tell you why," the tutor said. "I can't now. There is nothing I can do now. Like you, Rose, I am in bad trouble. Very bad trouble."

"You are helping me; will you let me help you?" she asked.

He lifted the hand he was holding to his lips and

kissed it. "Bless you," he said fervently. "But this is something I must do myself."

They had reached the west gate leading into the grounds of the Manor.

"Where is the combination?" he asked her.

There was only a fractional pause and then she dug her hand into her coat pocket and handed him a slip of paper. He turned his flashlight on it. He was so still that he seemed like a graven image. Then he said slowly, "I think you have given me the wrong memorandum."

She groped in her pocket again and found another folded slip of paper: 4L—2R—65L. He examined it carefully and then put it in his own pocket. "That's it," he said in a tone of satisfaction. "Good night, Rose. Go to sleep and don't worry. It will be all right."

It was not until she reached her own room that she remembered Mr. Smith had not returned the other piece of paper to her. What could it have been, she wondered, that interested him so deeply? And then she recalled that she had stuffed Craven's message into her pocket and given him that by mistake.

Suddenly it seemed desperately important that she should regain that incriminating piece of paper. She groped her way down the stairs in the dark and out into the garden. But Mr. Smith had gone. She dropped down on a corner of a rustic seat. It was bright moonlight. The shrubs cast fantastic shadows on the graveled paths. The carved face in the wall, from whose open mouth water dripped continually in summer, seemed to grin at her derisively. There was a constant rustle among the dry leaves. She listened intently.

What a variety of sound there was, if one took notice. The rustling branches of the trees made one tone; the dry twigs of the shrubs seemed to come together with a tinkle and clash as the slight wind swayed their frosted tips; the leaves on the ground gave out a rising and falling sound, constant, unceasing, like the ebbing and coming tide. In the distance a hound bayed the moon and near at hand another answered. The lights of the Manor glowed hospitably.

She went over and over in her mind her conversation with Mr. Smith. Even alone in the garden she was comforted by the memory of his strong hand clasping hers. Perhaps, after all, she had found a friend, a man who would risk danger for himself, even disgrace if he were discovered, to help her out of her difficulty. A man who said he too had known great trouble.

She pulled her coat more closely around her to keep out the autumn chill, thinking—wondering—dreaming. She had not known that a man could be unselfish, kind, protective.

Then a harsh thought, born of her bitter experiences, shattered the peace that had gradually relaxed her taut nerves. And suppose that Smith, like Mark Craven, cared only for his own interests. Suppose he wanted the formula for himself. What had she done? Oh, what had she done?

Her eyes moved wildly around the dark garden like a cornered animal seeking some means of escape.

Then Martha Mumford's face flashed into her mind. With a smothered exclamation she jumped to her feet, stealthily opened the creaking west gate and went swiftly down the road toward the village, keeping well within the shadow of the hedges which bordered estates along the way.

The little waffle shop was dark when she got there but Rose was too desperate to be balked now. She picked up a handful of pebbles and threw them against a window she surmised might be in a bedroom.

The stones had barely touched the pane and fallen to the ground again before the sash was raised and a crisp voice inquired, "What do you want?"

"Oh, Mrs. Mumford, it's Rose from the Manor. Please let me in."

It seemed ages to the terrified girl before a small

figure in a gray blanket robe held the door wide. "Come in, child. Come in. I've been expecting you for a long time."

An hour later, when Rose had finished a cup of hot chocolate and some of Martha Mumford's famous brownies, over her protest that she could not swallow a bite, the older woman spoke quietly. It was the first time she had attempted to speak since Rose had come in. She had listened in silence to the torrential outburst of words and tears and accusations. Then she had made her eat.

"And is that all?" she asked quietly.

"All!"

Martha smiled in answer to that bewildered exclamation. "I know," she said. "It seems to you like the end of the world."

"It *is* the end of the world for me."

"Don't talk nonsense," the old woman said sharply. "And I ask again, is that all? Is there anything you are holding back?"

"Nothing," the girl assured her.

"You have had a lot of trouble," Martha said slowly. "And some of it you have brought on yourself. But if you've made mistakes you've tried to make up for them and I think you are going to try even harder. Some day, if you remember all this—"

"I'll never forget it."

"You'd be surprised to know how many heartaches, how many bitter disappointments, how many disasters that seem final when they come, we learn to survive and in time even to forget. And I think, Rose, you'll be able to forget this."

The girl looked at her from wide eyes, filled with disbelief.

"But you can't simply rely on time," Martha told her. "It takes a lot of courage to face trouble. A lot of courage. But I believe you have it, Rose, or you wouldn't have fought at all. You would have given in and done the easiest thing."

"You—you believe in me?" the girl whispered.

"What matters," Martha Mumford said, "is that you must learn to believe in yourself. Now run along home and get some sleep. Tomorrow—well, now, I've a great mind to see what I can do tomorrow."

XI

The morning was everything a morning ought to be, sunny and clear and crisp. The sky was a brilliant blue vault and the air was electric, seeming to promise that only joy could come on such a day as this.

Beth dressed carefully. Her suitcases were already packed for the jaunt to New York. She should be very happy but instead she was thoughtful. What should she do about Stone? Should she tell Chris or Colonel Jim that the man masquerading as a butler was really a private detective? She remembered his warning: A human life is involved. Somehow she believed him. Suppose that idle or thoughtless words of hers should cause a real tragedy? Better not risk it. Anyhow, this was the first, the only time in her life when Chris had appointed himself her escort, had promised to attend her all day, all evening, all the next day, wherever she wanted to go, whatever she wanted to do.

Of course, she admitted to herself, he was doing it because he wanted to make clear to everyone that he was not interested in Evelyn; he wanted—though he did not tell her this out of delicacy and good taste —to save Evelyn the humiliation and himself the discomfort of having to make clear to her in blunt words that he did not want to renew the engagement.

And yet—suppose, Beth said to herself as she adjusted a hat on her bronze curls—suppose this were really our wonderful day, Chris's and mine; suppose he were planning to spend it with me because he preferred me to anyone else in the world. Well, she said defiantly to herself, if it is all pretense anyhow, for two days I am going to pretend that it is true. I'll have those two days to remember for the rest of my life, even if it is all I ever have.

She came flying down the stairs to breakfast and did the "Skater's Waltz" across the room to the buffet. The morning meal was a most informal affair at the Manor, each member of the family as he appeared helping himself from the various dishes which, in appetizing array, adorned the buffet.

"Oh, what a beautiful morning," she caroled, as she provided herself with a grapefruit and drew her chair close to Ted's. "Thanks, I can reach the sugar myself."

Ted whistled in appreciation. "You're terrific, Slim —pardon *me*, Miss Gilbert—you are radiant; you dazzle these eyes weary from the pursuit of knowledge. You are positively fey."

"I'm happy," she told him.

"You don't need to explain. That fact is simply bursting from your eyes. All I hope is that in your present mad mood you won't do some wild, impulsive thing without me to look after you."

"Croaking old raven!" the girl mocked him.

"The voice of experience," he said with the heavy sigh of a careworn man. "You are heading straight for trouble, young woman. You think you can wind Chris around your finger but with him for an escort you'd better watch your step. He hasn't seen you in action before, the way I have. He probably thinks you'll sit against the wall until he unbends enough to ask you to dance. He doesn't know that if there isn't already a stag line, it gets a mile long when you heave in sight. I know you—" with brotherly severity.

Her cheeks were a deep pink, her eyes glowed as she flouted him. "Anyone would think the Bradford men like wallflowers. I haven't seen the little Blossom holding up any walls at dances."

"That's different," Ted began, and then had to join in her laugh. "Hi, there, Chris. Had your breakfast? I hear you've been snared by this designing woman into taking a holiday. Keep your eyes on Slim. She's out for conquest; I can see it in her off eye."

Chris's eyes warmed as he looked at Beth, in a soft brown wool dress and a brown hat with a tiny russet feather that matched her hair.

"Don't listen to him, Chris," she laughed. "I plan to be a model of deportment. What else can I do," she added with a tragic sigh, "when I am under the stern eye of my guardian?"

"You might," he told her, "forget for once that I am your guardian."

Ted's eyes flashed from one to the other and he concealed a delighted grin behind his napkin.

"I suppose," Beth said, "before we can get started someone will come tearing in at the last moment, breathing hoarsely and gasping, 'Where's Chris? I must see Chris.'"

"Good morning," Anne Bradford said from the doorway. "Ted, I hate to leave you behind but—"

"But Smithy says I'm slow in mastering Spanish. Talk about slave drivers! Though he seems to be rather absentminded lately. I got by with doing Wednesday's lesson over again on Thursday and he never noticed it. Congratulated me on having it letter-perfect. Anyhow, don't worry about me. I am the family martyr. And you're going to have your hands full with Slim, unless I miss my guess. She's fey this morning."

Mrs. Bradford looked up. "What is it, Kate?" she asked as the maid appeared at the door. "Don't say it's a telephone call for Mr. Chris."

"No, ma'am. Cook and I were just saying the phone hasn't rung once this morning. But Cook would like to see you for a moment before you go."

"I'll see her at once. Then we'd better leave while our luck holds," Mrs. Bradford said as she left the room.

"Well, can you beat that," Ted exclaimed. "Not a telephone call this morning. I'll bet the widows and orphans have begun to get onto you, Chris, or something has happened to the telephone. Maybe I'd better investigate." He dropped his napkin in his chair and started for the door.

"Ted," Beth wailed. As Chris shot her a quick look she flushed vividly. "Put some more bread in the toaster for me, will you? You can attend to that old phone any time."

Ted examined her critically, his head on one side. "Go slow on those eats, Slim. Do I discern a slight pillow—I beg pardon, billow—under that classic chin? Is there a tendency to too, too solid flesh in yon lithe and willowy figure?"

Mrs. Bradford came back. "Chris, let's start at once. We must stop for Colonel Jim and it's a shame to lose one moment of this heavenly morning."

Anne Bradford was seated in the back of the car and Chris was about to start the motor when Beth, at his side, mumbled, "Forgot something! Back in a moment."

She ran to where Ted stood on the steps and thrust an envelope into his hand. Before the astonished boy could speak she was in her seat again.

"Hurry, Chris!" she exclaimed. "Hurry!"

As the car started she looked back. Ted was reading the slip of paper he had pulled from the envelope. He dropped it with a shout and made a megaphone of his hands.

"Chris! Chris!"

With a laugh of pure mischief Beth called back, "Too late! To-o la-te!" as the car swept from the driveway.

She settled down with a sigh of contentment beside Chris and looked at him out of the corner of her eye. He seemed different this morning, less stern, his eyes as eager as a boy's. He too seemed to be in a mood to make the most of his holiday.

"Wonderful morning for our jaunt," Colonel Jim exclaimed as he climbed into the car. "Anne, while Beth and Chris are playing around in New York I see no reason why you and I should not make some—"

"Some whoopee," Anne said gravely, using one of Ted's favorite terms, and they all laughed.

Wonderful. The word seemed pitifully inadequate to Beth as the car sped smoothly through the countryside. The world was redolent of morning freshness. In the shadowed places a light frost whitened the ground. The sky overhead spread like a huge sapphire. The dark, mysterious pines seemed to be whispering magic secrets as their tops swayed together above the other trees which had shed their foliage. Great heaps of fallen leaves showed russet, with an occasional touch of gold. The streams were like mirrors in their glassy stillness, and cattle wandered along the banks so near the water's edge that they appeared to be grazing nose to nose with their own black and white reflections.

The girl's heart fairly sang with happiness. Here was where she belonged. She was a part of the country as it was a part of her. The scheme of life which she had built for herself had been based upon country living, welcoming the recurring seasons, watching and supervising the growth of crops, feeling responsible for the land and its best use. But her scheme of life, she realized now, had been founded on the idea that she would never leave the Manor, that her work and interests would be there as well as her life.

What, she wondered, would have happened to her if her father had not left her in the care of the Bradford men?

"A penny for them," Chris said.

"I was thinking of my father. Thinking how hard it must have been to leave this beautiful world, all of a sudden, in the midst of his plans, almost on his way to success."

"He never knew what hit him," Chris tried to reassure her. He made the mistake of correcting his words. "That is, he just fell unconscious, you know, without pain."

"Never knew what hit him." Beth seized on the words. "Do you believe someone—deliberately—"

"Not today," Chris said quickly. "This is our day. It is not to be spoiled by gloomy thoughts."

"Our day," she repeated contentedly.

His low voice could not be heard on the back seat where Anne and Colonel Jim were chatting vivaciously with the ease of old and tried companions. "Happy?" he asked her.

"So happy, Chris." She slipped her hand under his arm and then withdrew it quickly. "Sorry," she said. "I know you don't like to have me do that when you are driving."

"I—I love it," he said unsteadily. His hand dropped from the wheel and covered hers. The tone of his voice sent her blood racing through her veins and her heart pounding in her throat. She tried firmly to tell herself that she was silly but she ignored the admonishing voice. This was her day, *their* day. She was not going to be sensible and that was all there was to it.

"You aren't acting like a guardian today, Chris," she said daringly.

"My duties as a guardian are almost over," he said, "now that you have grown up."

She laughed. "So at last you have discovered that I have grown up!"

"Yes, I've discovered it at last. But there is one matter on which my guardian's duties are still in force. You can't marry without my approval, you know."

"I shall make no promises," she answered gaily.

After they had settled in their hotel, Beth met Chris in the lobby according to plan.

"Where are we going?" she asked as he took her arm and led her out of the hotel.

He laughed. "That's my secret."

"A surprise!" she said gleefully. "Oh, Chris, what fun. Do you remember all the ways you used to surprise me when I was young?" He smiled quizzically down at her but there was something warm and tender behind the laughter. "I mean when I was a child."

Fifth Avenue looked incredibly prosperous and beautiful. Traffic moved in unbroken lines from the arch at Washington Square to 110th Street. Women strolled along the street, glancing at the magnificent windows. Beth was drawn to them as though by a magnet and Chris paused at her side, looking down at her radiant face and smiling at her pleasure.

"Tiffany's," she said, stopping enthralled to look at the jewelry gleaming like stars. "What beauty, Chris."

"Do jewels mean as much as that?" he asked. "I did not know you cared for them. You have never asked for them."

"Would a ward dare ask to purchase such magnificence? I can imagine your 'off-with-her-head' frown. And anyhow I am barbaric in my taste. I want a big splashy ring that reaches from here to there."

"Let's go in and buy one," he suggested.

"Chris, have you gone quite mad?"

"No, I am belatedly beginning to show symptoms of sanity. It's perfectly proper to accept a gift from your guardian. Come on in."

"Don't tempt me," she implored him. "Ted was right; I'm fey today; I'd do any crazy thing."

For answer he held open the door of the famous store. Like a man who is in familiar surroundings, he went directly to a counter displaying rings. A suave, prosperous-looking man bowed to him.

"Glad to see you back, Mr. Bradford."

Beth looked her surprise at the man's greeting. Chris was known here. Of course, he must have made many gifts to Evelyn. Not only the ring she was wearing so defiantly but other things. Beth crushed back a little jealous ache at her heart and forced her attention to what Bradford was saying.

"That tray of rings, I think." He smiled at Beth. "Splashy ones. Is that the word?"

As the man reached for the tray, Beth whispered doubtfully, "Is this right, Chris?"

"Can't you trust me, dear?"

She nodded dumbly and looked at the glittering mass spread before her. As she pounced upon a ring she exclaimed rapturously. In a setting of small diamonds blazed a yellow stone of marvelous brilliancy.

She slipped the gleaming thing on her finger and moved her hand back and forth under the light.

"It—it's bottled sunlight," she cried.

"Sure that is the one you want?"

"I've never loved anything so much. But it must be expensive."

"Does it fit?" He took her hand in his and moved the circlet up and down.

"Like a glove."

He drew a checkbook from his pocket and made out his check. While he was doing so, the clerk warned Beth, "Be careful with that ring. It's one of the finest yellow diamonds I have ever seen."

As Chris handed him the check, the salesman looked from the smiling man to the enraptured girl. "Thank you, Mr. Bradford, and may I offer my congratulations? I hope you will both be very happy."

The color flamed in Beth's cheek but Chris only laughed and thanked him. When they were on the street he ignored the incident.

"Christopher Bradford," Beth said breathlessly, "you've given me a yellow diamond. The man said so."

He laughed and tucked her hand under his arm. "Just the ring I had my eyes on. I came into New York several days ago, looked around, introduced myself, and picked that one out for you, but I thought you might like to make your own choice."

That night they made a merry foursome at Pierre's, where Beth displayed her ring proudly.

Anne's eyes glowed with delight but before she could comment, Chris forestalled her by saying quickly, "High time my ward had a gift. This is to celebrate our having a holiday in the big city."

Colonel Jim glanced at his watch. "I'd much rather stay right where we are, but if we are going to make an appearance at Maizie Towle's whindig—"

"On our way," Beth said breezily, more breezily than she felt. For a moment the brilliancy of the diamond was dimmed.

"What is it," Chris asked under his breath as he

helped her into the taxi under the awning. "Changed your mind about the ring?"

Did he suspect that she minded the fact that it was only a token of celebrating a holiday? Had he guessed how she felt about him? He must not know. Her heart fluttered. Steadied.

"It's just right," she assured him. "Anyhow, if Evelyn is still wearing your—her—ring I may as well be wearing one that she can see."

"Evelyn?" Chris shrugged his shoulders. "Let's forget about Evelyn."

But Chris had not heard Evelyn's declaration of war the day before, had not seen the cold menace in her eyes when she left Mrs. Bradford's drawing room.

The party, on a hotel roof, was already in full swing when they arrived, a brilliant affair with a famous orchestra playing lilting music, with the gleam of shoulders and the sparkle of jewels and the fragrance of flowers.

When she had left her wrap and paused for a moment in the powder room to look at her reflection—a slim girl in yellow chiffon that left her shoulders bare, with her bronze hair swept up over her ears in soft waves, and her mother's diamond earrings, the yellow diamond gleaming on her left hand—Beth started toward the ballroom.

She had to stop beside some massed chrysanthemums because the passageway ahead was blocked by three girls who had gathered in a small group to talk. Rather than push past them she waited for a moment, and above the lilting strains of a tango she heard a girl's urgent whisper.

"I tell you I won't be made a fool of!"

"My dear, you are upset. There was never any intention of making a fool of you." The man's voice was low, but not low enough to conceal a note of infinite boredom.

"You made me think you were in love with me."

"Love," the man said reflectively. "Somehow I don't think love enters much into your calculations."

"Then you are simply going to drop me like—"

"Don't say, 'like an old glove.' Clichés are rather trying." This time the man's contempt was too obvious for even the angry girl to miss.

"All right," she said venomously. "Now I know where I stand. I'll know what to do now."

Beth caught her breath. That was Evelyn speaking. Evelyn and who else? Chris? No, Chris would never speak like that to any woman, even a woman whom he disliked. The little group ahead melted away and Beth hastened past the massed chrysanthemums to the spot where Anne stood. At a little distance, Colonel Jim and Chris were waiting for them.

Together they went down the reception line. Then, as Ted had foretold, Beth was swept away, besieged by partners, and carried off to the dance floor. Chris looked after her blankly; he had fully intended to have the first dance with her himself.

Seeing his expression, Anne Bradford's face lighted up in a mischievous smile. "I've been telling you for two years, Chris, that the child is incredibly lovely and extremely popular. It's like this wherever she goes. There are always strings of boys and men waiting to cut in when she is dancing."

Chris drew back to the edge of the crowd, watching Beth as she danced lightly as a feather, laughing, waving, fending off admiring comments, enjoying herself as wholeheartedly as a child, without coquetry, without seeming conscious of her beauty or the effect she had on people. She could scarcely move more than a few steps with any partner before another cut in.

How could I have been so blind, Chris thought. She is barely twenty-two and lovely and popular. Naturally she prefers boys of her own age. No wonder she thinks I am staid and old. But it's not too late, he decided, setting his jaw. There's still time to make her see that I am young and have as great a capacity for gaiety as these boys.

He started toward her but checked himself. A tall blond man, in superbly tailored evening clothes, had suavely and deftly sidestepped the stag line and claimed Beth.

Mark Craven again! Mark Craven seemed to crop up wherever Beth was. Chris searched the girl's face as Craven swept her past him, dancing well as he seemed to do everything. Beth's face was alight with interest in what he was saying to her. Chris growled to himself, aware of his jealousy but helpless to cope with it. Craven was a polished man of the world, sophisticated, entertaining. No wonder he could attract Beth, as he had attracted Julia Seagreave and Evelyn Furnas.

A hand touched his arm. "Dreaming, Chris?"

He turned to find Evelyn Furnas standing beside him. "Good evening, Evelyn."

"Darling," she protested. "Anyone would think we were strangers."

"I thought you wanted it that way?" he replied coolly. He looked down at the hand clutching his arm so tenaciously, saw his ring sparkling on her finger.

"Chris!" The china-blue eyes smiled up into his. "Dance with me. We always dance so well together. Or have you forgotten?"

He led her out onto the floor. "I want to talk to you," she said.

When she was silent, swaying in his arms in time to the music, he prodded with a faint note of impatience in his voice, "Well?"

"It's terribly important, darling, and yet I almost forget when I am dancing with you. In white tie and tails you are really devastating, Chris."

He made no comment, turning, sidestepping, backing, moving with the lilt of the dance band. At length, wondering at the silence of the usually loquacious Evelyn, he looked down and saw that her eyes were intent, but not on him. He followed their direction. Craven was dancing past, laughing at something Beth was saying. Beth's hand rested on his arm, and on her fourth finger blazed the yellow diamond.

Evelyn drew in her breath with a hissing sound.

"So that's it," she muttered. "I might have known. Let's get out of this crowd where we can talk, Chris. There's a lot you ought to know."

He followed her out on the terrace. "Cold?" he asked with a glance at her bare shoulders and feeling the icy sweep of the wind through his heavier clothing.

She shrugged impatiently. "It doesn't matter, Chris, did you see the ring your ward is wearing?"

"Yes, I—"

"I suppose Mark Craven gave it to her. Well, it's time you knew the truth about him, Chris. He came here to work his way into the Manor because he wants the Gilbert formula. And if the only way he can get it is to marry the Gilbert girl, he'll take her with it. Don't trust him, Chris."

"I don't trust him," Chris told her quietly.

"Oh, why," she said, her voice breaking, "did I ever let you go?" She stretched out her hands to him pleadingly, and when he did not take them, her arms crept around his neck. "Chris," she cried. "Darling, take me back."

A broad path of golden light spilled over them as the doors from the ballroom opened and a couple came out. Craven and Beth. Chris gently detached Evelyn's hands from around his neck, his eyes on Beth in an unspoken message.

"Sorry, Evelyn," he said crisply. "Wrong time. Wrong station. You see, that is my diamond Beth is wearing."

XII

"What heavenly music," Beth exclaimed.

Craven, moving with expert ease, smiled down at her. "I believe you could dance to the music of the spheres," he said. He steered her dexterously away from the stag line. "Now that I have you I intend to keep you."

Below the laughing threat there was an earnestness that would not be ignored. Beth freed herself from the too close pressure of his arms, studying him in swift sidelong glances as they swirled around the ballroom. Little as she liked echoing Julia's ideas, she admitted to herself, reluctantly, that he was an impressive man.

"Tell me, Miss Gilbert, why is it so difficult to see you? Whenever I call—morning, noon and night—you always seem to be busy."

"There is so much to do—so many people to see. I have been away a long time, you know. And besides, I help Chris in small ways with the management of his estate."

"That sounds like a full schedule," he admitted, smiling as he caught her questioning glance. "But just the same I wish you would make time in it for me." When she found no immediate reply, he asked with a directness that took her aback, "There isn't anything about me that you particularly dislike, is there?"

"Good heavens, no," she replied with a laugh.

"Then," he said triumphantly, "I'm going to make you like me very much—very, very much."

Something in his tone made Beth feel ill at ease. For once she found it difficult to maintain the gay, easy impersonality she preferred when dancing. Mark

Craven was not a college boy, he was a mature man. He knew what he wanted and he was not to be put off lightly.

"Though I see," he added, "that I'll have to work against obstacles. Like those road signs: Proceed at your own risk. Fortunately for me, I am not easily frightened off."

Beth laughed spontaneously. "Do you find me frightening, Mr. Craven?"

He smiled down at her. "The name is Mark," he reminded her. "No, I don't find *you* frightening. Your threat is to my heart and I am ready to risk that." Again his tone made her uncomfortable. He sounded as though he meant it; he was much too serious for ballroom conversation. She ignored his last comment.

"You don't find me frightening? Who then?"

"I said," he corrected, "that I am not easily frightened. Or discouraged. After all, you are of age, you are independent. Some day you will break those bonds that—"

"What bonds?"

"How many girls of your age," Craven asked, "are guarded as you are—so that they can't break away? Guarded. Does it ever occur to you that your guardian takes that word rather literally?"

"But I am free, Mr. Craven," Beth protested.

"Are you?" His colorless eyes probed hers. No, Beth thought, I am not free. It is true that Chris guards me like a watchdog, checks on everything I do. And yet— she looked up at Craven's face but for once he was not looking at her. His eyes were fixed on the doors leading out onto the balcony.

"Miss Gilbert—Beth," he said abruptly. "Sometimes I wonder whether Bradford is not the one who is responsible for your refusing all my invitations. Surely you are of age."

"Of course I am," she flamed. "And I am responsible for my own actions, Mr. Craven. Chris's authority exists only in one thing—he has the right to approve of the man I marry."

"Mr. Bradford is a far-seeing man," Craven said

dryly. "Never underestimate the power of a—guardian. It is warm in here. Let's go out on the balcony and take a look at the city lights. From this height the view should be magnificent."

His hand under her arm was warm and possessive, too possessive, she thought, as he led her toward the balcony. A man and woman stood there, the woman's arms linked around the man's neck. Beth recognized Chris's dark head before he turned. Then she heard him say crisply, "Sorry, Evelyn. Wrong time. Wrong station. You see, that is my diamond Beth is wearing."

The interval that followed was absolutely silent and yet it seemed to be filled with the rumble of thunder, the crackle of lightning. Then Evelyn's arms dropped to her sides. She was unbelievably white. Only her blue eyes flamed, seeming to give off a mist like dry ice.

Her expression as she turned to Beth was so menacing that Chris instinctively took a step forward, standing protectively between the two girls. But Evelyn did not move. Unexpectedly she laughed.

"This deal is yours," she said. "But the game isn't played out. Not by a long shot."

Chris held out his hand to Beth. "Our dance, dear. I haven't had a chance all evening."

Reluctantly Craven relinquished her, patting his face, a trifle too florid from dancing, with a flamboyantly monogrammed handkerchief.

"All right, Bradford. But, as Miss Furnas pointed out, the game isn't over yet. My time will come." With a queer smile he turned abruptly and left the balcony.

"Now what did he mean by that cryptic utterance, Chris?" Beth asked.

"Theatrical claptrap," Chris said briefly. His face was troubled. "Sorry you had to be let in for that scene with Evelyn. Do you mind terribly?"

"I was sorry for her," Beth admitted slowly. "I couldn't help it." But in her loyalty to her own sex, she did not tell Chris that this was the second time in one evening that Evelyn had been rejected. The girl's humiliation must be unbearable, and yet—and yet, Beth had to admit to herself, a girl who attempted to force two reluctant men to marry her within a few hours could not be very deeply involved emotionally. Whatever was at stake, Evelyn's heart was not touched.

For a moment they stood side by side, looking out and down over the fantastic vista, over millions of lights creating a fairy-tale city against the dark night; the gleam of black rivers arched by bridges that seemed to float on light, brilliant towers thrusting into the sky; the glare of Broadway making a white patch against the night; the muted roar of motors in a city that never slept, never was still.

"Lovely," she whispered. "How lovely."

"Do you like it so much?"

"More than I can say. But not for always. For tonight. It belongs to tonight."

"And what would you want for always?" he asked tenderly.

"The country," Beth said simply. "Changing seasons, and fields that bear crops and are harvested and are blanketed with snow. Peace and a sense of growing things."

"We like the same things, don't we, Beth? We always have."

She nodded, her bronze curls brushing his shoulder. For a moment his arms went around her and then he turned swiftly.

"Let's dance," he said, and led her back into the brilliantly lighted ballroom.

This was not like dancing with Craven, expert as he was. It seemed to Beth that she floated in Chris's arms.

"Do you know," he said, "this is the first time you've ever danced with me?"

Beth tilted back her head laughing. "Do you know it's the first time you ever asked me?" she retorted. "You wouldn't waste your time on a kid."

"Can't you forget that? I grovel, I apologize, I am contrite, I see the error of my ways."

Beth smothered a ripple of laughter. "Well, as long as you seem properly apologetic."

Then, as his arm tightened, she fell silent, content merely with the movement of the dance, the polished floor, the music, the exquisite dresses floating past, Chris's arm holding and guiding her. She closed her eyes, shut in with her dreams and her contentment. Her heart was pounding. Suppose Chris noticed it?

She made an effort to break the spell that bound her. "Chris," she said, speaking lightly, "I have a horrible confession to make. Perhaps I'd better tell you here. You wouldn't dare beat me in public, would you?"

For a moment he missed a step. She looked up to see that he had lost color, that his mouth was sternly set.

"Chris," she protested. "What are you thinking? I only wanted to confess that I stuffed all the telephone bells at the Manor with paper early this morning so that no one could call you and delay our trip."

He caught her close with a force that almost took her breath, the color surging back into his face, his eyes glowing down into hers.

"Beth—Beth, I have a horrible confession to make." He mimicked her tone. "I saw you do it."

"Chris!"

"I knew what was in the note you gave Ted," he teased her. "Instructions to unmuzzle the bells."

"Christopher Bradford, you are a wizard—you—" She finished her sentence with an irrepressible laugh in which he joined her. A young laugh. A boy's laugh.

"And you are Titania, queen of the fairies. Or at least you dance like her. What a blind fool I was not to have—"

"Have what?" she asked when he paused abruptly.

"Have danced with you before," he said, but that was not what he had started to say.

It was a wonderfully comforting feeling to have Chris's arms about her. What was there about him that made her so blissfully content to be with him?

"Tired, Beth?" he asked gently.

"Of course not. I have an idea—"

"I have an idea," he began at the same moment and stopped with a laugh. "Ladies first."

"I was thinking of a perfect way of rounding off our wonderful day," she said. "A ride through Central Park in a hansom cab."

"I told you we liked the same things." He was triumphant. "That was my idea too."

The usual line of hansom cabs was drawn up at the entrance to Central Park outside the Plaza Hotel. Chris selected the cleanest one and the elderly driver, wearing the traditional silk hat tilted over one eye, helped them in and seated himself on his high box.

After the brilliant lights they plunged into cool darkness and a quiet broken only by the leisurely clop-clop of the horse, which ambled along. This was one ride on which no one was ever in a hurry.

As they made the slow circuit, Beth saw first the lights of Fifth Avenue, then those of the great apartment buildings on Central Park West, and finally those of Central Park South, with the brilliant lights of Broadway at the right. She did not attempt to speak. Above the trees, stark now for their winter rest, waiting for coming snows to blanket them and keep them warm, rose the moon, cold and serene above the world.

Chris drew Beth's hand within his arm and the headlights of a passing car drew flames from the ring on her finger.

"That is my diamond Beth is wearing." Beth heard Chris's voice as he had spoken to Evelyn.

"Chris," she said, hoping he would not notice the unsteadiness in her voice, "are we to keep up this—farce—about our engagement?"

"Farce?" he said blankly. Then he caught himself. "Yes," he said expressionlessly. "For a little while."

"Why?" she demanded. "Because of Evelyn? Because of Mark Craven? Because—"

"Because?" he asked eagerly.

"Because of my father's formula?" she asked, as

though something inside her had spoken the words without her volition.

"Because—for your protection," Chris said. "You can trust me, Beth. This is the best way."

It is the best way, he told himself defiantly. The only way I know how to protect her. Someone followed her in Europe and searched her belongings at the Manor. Under my very eyes! From that moment I've known she was in danger. Someone killed her father to find that formula. Someone—ice crawled up his spine. His fingers closed over the slim hand that wore the glittering ring.

Beth gave a sharp exclamation.

"Chris! I was just staring idly at the trees and thinking how neat they are compared with those at home, no underbrush growing wild under them, and suddenly—it came to me where I'd seen poison ivy at the Manor. There's a vine that keeps growing up around one of the pillars of the balcony outside Mr. Smith's room. That's where he must have got it. Only —" Her voice trailed off.

"Only why," Chris asked, "would Smith be climbing up the pillar of the balcony instead of going in and out of the house by means of the staircase?"

"Queer, isn't it?" she asked.

"Very queer indeed."

A car passed them, going at terrific speed, straight toward the headlights of an advancing car. With an exclamation the driver of the hansom pulled on the reins, stopping the horse. But nothing could stop the car. It crashed into the oncoming one with a splintering sound, and above it rose screams.

"Don't look," Chris said, catching Beth in his arms, hiding her face against his shoulder.

"Is it—are they—"

The screams had stopped.

"I'm afraid so," he said quietly. "Stay here, my darling. I'll see if there is anything—"

"No." Beth was shaking violently but her voice was decisive. "I don't run away from trouble. I'll go with you. Perhaps I can help."

By the time they reached the wreck, other cars had gathered, those in black honking their horns in irritation at a delay, however slight. With a screaming siren a radio car drew up. While one of the policemen held back the crowd the other investigated.

His face was white when he turned around. "All dead," he said. "Move on. Move on. Drunk, from the smell in that car."

In answer to Chris's inquiry, he said there was nothing to be done. An ambulance would take care of the bodies.

The driver of the hansom cab turned his horse and they went back toward the lights of Central Park South, Chris holding Beth tenderly in his arms while she sobbed against his shoulder.

"They were—were so terribly young," she sobbed. "Think of their mo—mothers. Our wonderful day will be a day of—of such sorrow for other people."

"Every day," Chris reminded her, "is a day of birth and of death, of marriage and divorce, of hope and despair for someone. When our griefs come we will be able, I hope, to face them with courage, but when our joys come, when one wonderful day is ours, let's not darken it."

He smiled down at her. "The cabby will take us back to the hotel. We are on Fifth Avenue now. Wipe off those tears and have a smile ready."

He put his handkerchief into her groping hand and she wiped her eyes, sat up straighter and smoothed back her hair, summoning up a tremendous smile.

In the hotel lobby they saw Colonel Jim, wearing his evening clothes as though they were a uniform, his bearing as erect as when he had served in the army. He was pacing up and down, so engrossed in his thoughts that he did not see them until Chris touched his arm.

"Have you had a pleasant evening?" Chris asked.

"What's that—oh—er—yes."

"Has Mother gone up to her room?"

"Just a few minutes ago. Chris, I—well—"

"You finally asked her!" Chris exclaimed.

Colonel Jim nodded. "I asked Anne to be my wife."

"I am glad, more glad than I can say, sir." Chris held out his hand.

Colonel Jim took it in his. "Thank you, my boy. My —son. If only—It's hard to wait, you know. Darned hard."

Wait for what, Beth wondered, as Chris took her up in the elevator. The sitting room of their suite was empty and there was no light under Nan Bradford's door.

Beth turned to Chris. "Thank you for my wonderful day." She held out both hands to him.

He took them in his, looking down at her, his eyes intent, probing hers.

"Beth—" he began huskily. His mouth curved in a smile. "You are half asleep," he laughed. "You must go to bed at once. I won't keep you up a moment longer. The sleeping beauty, Craven called you. What was the charm that awakened her? Oh, yes." He bent over, drew her to him gently, and his mouth brushed her lips, lightly, tenderly. Then he said, "Good night," and went out before she could speak.

XIII

Beth Gilbert lay awake in her hotel room. After the soothing quiet and darkness of her room at the Manor, she was disturbed by the reflection of car lights moving across the ceiling, the muted sound of automobile horns and motors many floors below, the muffled, ceaseless rumble of the city.

But these things disturbed her only vaguely. The pressure of Chris's lips still tingled on her own. Chris, she murmured, Chris. With her right hand she felt for the ring on her left hand with its big stone, raised it to her cheek and held it there. She was not thinking; she was dreaming of Chris's eyes, his voice, his beautifully shaped brown hands, the touch of his lips.

When she slept at last she dreamed of him still, dreamed that he held her close in his arms and told her over and over again that he loved her. The intensity of her own emotion awakened her.

For a few moments the spell of the dream held her. Then it faded like dissolving fog. Still half asleep, half awake, she lay motionless, letting thoughts drift through her mind as they would. She remembered Evelyn's anguished conversation with some man at the party. Had that been Craven? Probably. Even the man-hunting Evelyn would hardly attempt to capture three men at one time. Beth remembered Chris saying in a voice she had never heard before, "You see, that is my diamond Beth is wearing."

Then she saw Mark Craven with that queer smile on his face, heard his voice saying, "My time will come." Mark Craven. He believed that Chris was behaving more like a warden in charge of a prisoner than like a guardian looking after a ward. He believed that Chris, for hidden reasons of his own, was trying to prevent her from seeing him. He believed Chris had some purpose in declaring that Beth could not marry without his approval.

Beth, who had always slept as soundly as a small child, tossed and turned, plumped up her pillows, moved restlessly. Why wouldn't Chris explain his reasons for guarding her so closely? For the worst of it was that Craven was right when he pointed out that Chris was guarding her. But why? Why? He put her off when she wanted a reason. Not now, he had told her; trust me. It's for your protection.

Into her mind flashed the warning words of Stone, Colonel Haswell's mysterious butler-detective. *A human life is involved.* But whose life—whose? And had that any connection with Chris's surveillance over her? Had it anything to do with being shadowed in Europe?

Sleep began to jumble her thoughts, to blur them, to mix them up. She thought mistily of the poison ivy that grew around the pillar under Smith's balcony. *A human life is involved.* Colonel Haswell saying, "It's hard to wait." The man lurking in the garden at the Manor, a big man with thick shoulders and a gleaming bald head. Chris saying, "He never knew what hit him."

Her eyelids closed. Beth was asleep. She slept while the sky turned light and then blue, while men and women in evening dress gave place to workmen in overalls and then to a million young men and women thronging the subways and the busses and the taxis on their way to offices. She slept when there was a tap at the door. She slept when a key moved smoothly in the lock and the door opened noiselessly and someone leaned over the bed, looking down at the tousled bronze curls and flushed cheeks, the closed eyes with their extravagantly long lashes. She slept when someone slipped silently out of the room, closing the door with only the faintest click.

In another room of the hotel the telephone rang and Colonel Haswell answered it.

"Hello. . . . This is Colonel Haswell speaking. . . . Yes, Mrs. Altman. You say Stone went out last night and has not returned? Did he take his luggage with him? . . . Nothing is gone? Did he receive any telephone calls before he left? . . . I see. No, don't call the police. Don't mention Stone's departure to anyone. He may simply have taken advantage of my absence to see some of his friends. He will probably return during the day. In any case, I'll be back some time this afternoon. . . . You didn't disturb me and it was quite proper to report it. I am sorry, too, to end my little holiday jaunt. Good-by, Mrs. Altman."

The colonel put down the phone, thought for a moment and then rang Chris's room. The latter answered immediately.

"Of course, Colonel. I'll be with you in a few moments. Mother and Beth will probably sleep late. Why not meet me downstairs for breakfast?"

When Chris stepped out of the elevator a quarter of an hour later, he took one look at Colonel Haswell's face and the cheery morning greeting died on his lips.

"Something has happened," he said quickly. "We'll order breakfast. You can tell me about it over the coffee."

When the waiter had removed the covers from crisp bacon and eggs and buttered toast and refilled their cups with coffee, he moved away to another table.

The colonel leaned forward, speaking in a low voice that would not carry to the next table. "My housekeeper, Mrs. Altman, telephoned this morning. Stone left the house without a word to her last night and he has not returned."

"So," Chris said thoughtfully, "things are beginning to move at last."

"Do you know what is happening?" the colonel asked curiously.

"I have an idea," Chris admitted.

"You know, I went into the whole thing blindfolded. I'm not sure I understand what is going on. Don't misunderstand me, Chris. I don't want to force your confidence. I'll do anything I can, in any case. But I might be more useful if I had an inkling as to what is about to happen."

"Thank you, Colonel. I appreciate your faith in me."

"Don't be absurd," the colonel said quickly. "Anyone who lacked faith in you, knowing you as I do, should have his head examined."

Chris smiled faintly. "The thing is this. Gilbert developed a new and revolutionary formula for plastics. The last night of his life he was setting out for New York with the formula in his pocket to show it to a man—unknown to me—who was to be his partner in developing it. Gilbert never reached New York. He was knocked down and robbed in our driveway and later died from the blow without regaining consciousness. That same night, the only other man who knew anything about the formula, his assistant, Larry Sergent, vanished from the face of the earth.

"As you know, I have spent the past two years trying to run down Sergent. A month ago, I announced publicly that I planned to manufacture the formula myself. That was an attempt to smoke the man out."

The colonel spread marmalade on his toast and poured another cup of coffee.

"And you believe," he said, "that Stone, who so opportunely appeared on the scene and applied for the job of my butler, is the man we are after? That he is the missing assistant, Larry Sergent?"

"I don't know," Chris admitted.

"What puzzles me," the colonel told him, "is why, if Sergent murdered Gilbert in order to get the formula for himself, he did not manufacture it. Why he simply vanished."

"If he had dared put the formula on the market," Chris said grimly, "I'd have had him arrested for murder."

"But what happened to the man?" the colonel insisted. "People simply can't disappear without a trace."

Chris laughed without mirth. "Sergent did. However, since that announcement appeared, stating that

I was going to manufacture the formula, there have
been indications that someone is working against me."
He repeated Martha Mumford's story about the rumors that had been spread concerning Chris having
acquired the formula by dishonest means. Haswell
muttered angrily. "The only person I could see," Chris
concluded, "who might have had any hand in spread-
ing that gossip was Stone. But since that time, there
have been other things." He described the odd behavior of Ted's tutor.

"Ted thinks Smith is a fine fellow," Haswell pointed
out, "and I must say I've liked the little I have seen
of him. But I know you too well to believe I have
to warn you to be sure of your facts before you do
anything that will injure an innocent man."

Chris went on to describe Smith's hands poisoned
with ivy which grew on the pillar under his balcony;
his surreptitious meeting with someone at the west
gate and the clever way in which he had called Chris's
attention to his own presence there and thus enabled
the other man to escape.

"And at the same time, as you know, Rose had an
appointment there with Mark Craven. The whole
thing is becoming too complicated for me. There are
too many people involved. I have had my eye on
Rose for some time. In case she had been planted
here by anyone interested in the formula, I deliberately staged that conversation with you for her benefit and left the combination of the safe where she
could not fail to find it. On the other hand, Colonel
Jim, she may simply represent some get-rich-the-easy-
way person who would like to try for the formula and
who had nothing to do with Gilbert's death. And what
I am after is the man who killed Beth's father. Because, until he is found, Beth is in danger."

"Not such danger," the colonel expostulated, "as
to whiten your lips that way."

"I can't be sure," Chris groaned.

"Oh," the older man said, enlightened. "So that's
it. You're in love with her."

"In love," Chris repeated, broodingly. "Those words

are used so much for so little. And what Beth means to me—"

"I know. And I must say, Chris, she is one in a million. Not just because she is beautiful and unspoiled and has a sweet temper and a fine intelligence. But there's a quality of—oh, call it courage and laughing gallantry and a delicate sense of honor. When she lifts those long curling eyelashes and you get a glimpse of her eyes you see something so direct, such clear depths, that you know this is a girl who can be trusted under any and every circumstance." Haswell cleared his throat. "Of course, Anne and I had been hoping lately—especially when she wore your ring last night—that you two young people had come to an understanding. Though Anne got the impression from Ted that it was just a maneuver to ward off Evelyn."

"Actually," Chris said, "it was a maneuver to ward off Mark Craven, though I didn't put it to Beth that way."

"I really believe you are letting your imagination get out of control in regard to Beth. After all, there is nothing anyone can do to her. And no reason for taking such a chance."

"Beth," Chris pointed out, "inherited the formula, if and when it is found."

"Well," Haswell said thoughtfully, "we can eliminate Craven. He did not follow Beth through Europe. He was here at the inn all summer. Stone? Smith? Even Rose? It would be interesting to know whether anyone else has taken advantage of our absence to—"

Chris pushed aside his untasted breakfast. "If you have finished, Colonel Jim, let's get to a telephone." Chris did not wait to go up to his own room. He went into a telephone booth in the lobby and called the Manor.

It was Ted who answered.

"That you, Chris? Say, did you ever find out why the telephone didn't ring before you left yesterday? Beth cooked up a scheme—"

"She told me. Have you been working hard? Is your tutor keeping you at it?"

"As a matter of fact," Ted said with a delighted chuckle, "I'm having an unscheduled holiday myself. Smithy seems to have gone off somewhere so I am going to try out my new car."

"You say Smith went off this morning?"

Something in Chris's voice made Ted say defensively, "Gee, he's worked like a trouper up until now. He rates a day off. No, he didn't go this morning. Matter of fact, I don't know just when he left. I found he was gone when I went to his room late last night. I didn't know what to do about Rose and I—"

"What's that about Rose?"

"I guess she just had a nightmare. I went into your study to get a dictionary—believe it or not, I worked on that Spanish until eleven o'clock—and darned if she wasn't sound asleep on the floor in front of your safe. When I tried to wake her up she began to yell, 'Don't do it.' I thought she might be out of her mind or something and I went for Smith but he wasn't around. She's all right this morning, though. Served breakfast, looked pale but said she was feeling fine. She said she used to walk in her sleep when she was a little girl and she guessed that was what had happened this time."

Chris made up his mind quickly. "Ted," he said, "I'll be back on the next train. I'm leaving the car for Mother and Beth. Don't tell anyone I am coming, will you?"

"If you don't want me to," Ted said, bewildered. "I might know you wouldn't stay away from the job for two whole days." He added in disgust, "After all, it isn't as though anything had happened to bring you back."

Elizabeth Gilbert slept until far into the morning. When she awakened, a clear, cold November breeze was fluttering the curtains at the windows, the sun shone with dazzling brilliancy. She looked at her traveling clock which ticked faithfully on the bedside table. Eleven o'clock. What a waste to sleep away a morning in New York!

She sat up, slid her feet into turquoise satin mules and pulled a matching robe of quilted satin over her white crepe pajamas. For a moment she stood at one of the windows looking down on Park Avenue, on the giant towers sparkling in the sun and the lines of traffic below. At length she turned reluctantly away and started her bath. When she had bathed and dressed in a beautifully cut black suit and brushed her hair until it shone, she put down the brush and noticed for the first time a square white envelope lying on her dresser. Had it been there when she went to bed the night before? No, she saw that it lay half covering the earrings she had worn to the dance. Then had it been left while she was taking her bath? The door of her room leading onto the hallway was locked. Perhaps Nan—

She ran across the sitting room that divided the two bedrooms and knocked at Anne Bradford's door. There was no response. She turned back uncertainly and saw a note scrawled in familiar writing on a piece of hotel stationery propped up on the desk.

You were so sound asleep, Mrs. Bradford had written, *that I had not the heart to wake you. Will return in time for luncheon at one-thirty. Chris was called back unexpectedly to the Manor. Nan.*

Chris gone! For a moment the girl felt as though the bottom had dropped out of the world. What could have called him home after he had made all arrangements to stay? Perhaps—the color flooded her face, then receded, leaving it pale—perhaps he suspected that she loved him and he had gone away to make her realize that he did not care for her.

Very serious, very tragic, very youthful, she threw her silver fox fur about her shoulders. The telephone rang. Mrs. Seagreave was in the lobby and would like to see Mrs. Bradford.

"Mrs. Bradford will not return until one-thirty," Beth said, "but tell Mrs. Seagreave that Miss Gilbert will be glad to see her if she cares to come up."

While she waited for Julia she put down her handbag and gloves and saw the square white envelope she was still carrying. She ripped it open. On a piece of cheap paper, letters from a newspaper had been cut out and pasted to form a message:

WHO KILLED YOUR FATHER AND STOLE HIS FORMULA?

XIV

Who killed your father and stole his formula? Beth's first instinctive feeling was to reject the message as a hoax, one of those "Fly at once; all is discovered" messages which appeal to people of primitive intelligence as being funny. But she didn't know anyone who would do such a thing.

Who killed your father and stole his formula? It's not true, she told herself firmly; it's an ugly thing someone is doing to frighten me, but it's not true. And then in her memory she heard Chris's voice saying, "He never knew what hit him."

A voice that was not her voice spoke in her ear. "How did he know?" it said.

A tap on the door was followed by Julia Seagreave, wearing an extravagant hat and a pale blue suit of youthful cut, carrying over her arm a short mink cape.

"Where is Anne?" she asked as she came into the living room.

"I—I don't know," Beth said from between dry lips. "I slept late and found a message. She has gone out. She'll be back at one-thirty for luncheon."

Julia's eyes swept over the girl. "I must say," she commented in a tone that did not conceal her satisfaction, "you look simply ghastly. Late hours don't suit you. Where's Chris?"

"He was called back unexpectedly to the Manor. He left this morning. On business of some kind, I suppose."

"How exasperating! At least, I expected Anne would be here. She knew perfectly well that I wanted her to go shopping with me. But I suppose—poor Anne!" Her tone fairly dripped sympathy.

"What's wrong?" Beth asked, trying to steady her seething thoughts, her reeling mind.

Julia shot her a quick glance from protuberant blue eyes. "As though you don't know! I simply can't decide what to do. There's no sense in waiting if she is going to be gone for *hours*. And I am rushed to death with fittings and committee meetings. And I did want Chris to look at a picture I am thinking of buying. I saw you at the Towle party last night. A choice mixture of sheep and goats, wasn't it? But then, what can one expect? The Towles are so terribly *new* themselves."

As Beth swayed on her feet, Julia went on impatiently. "For heaven's sake, sit down! You look as though you were going to faint. I suppose you've been dieting and gone to extremes on it. As soon as I saw how slim you were I thought you had been up to something like that. My dear, men simply *hate* women who are always swooning away. Better to put on a few pounds than look completely *washed out*."

Still Beth did not speak. Julia flounced around the room. "I don't know how Anne always manages to get the most attractive suite," she complained. "I wish you could see the slip covers in mine. Faded, my dear. Absolutely faded. I suppose Colonel Haswell is with Anne."

"I don't know," Beth said.

"For heaven's sake, why doesn't she marry the poor man and get it over? He has been hanging around her for centuries. Poor dear, she knows so little about men, or she'd have had him proposing long ago."

Beth, stunned with shock and angered by Julia's words, answered indiscreetly, "He has proposed."

"Oh," Julia said. "I don't understand why nobody thought of mentioning it to me." After a moment's consideration, she added, "Oh, of course. Poor dears."

"Why?"

"Oh, don't be such an innocent, Beth! That's all right for men. They simply eat it up. But, after all, I am another woman and it is wasted on me."

Remember Julia, Beth thought, and don't be angry.

She managed to say quietly, "I don't know what on earth you are talking about."

"No? It would be rather embarrassing for you, wouldn't it, if Anne were to marry and leave the Manor. You couldn't very well live in Chris's house without her, could you, even if he is your guardian. Why do you suppose Anne is postponing her happiness? Certainly not because she expects to grow any younger, or the poor, patient colonel either."

Beth looked at her speechlessly, her color ebbing until she was as white as though all the blood had drained out of her body.

"In some ways," Julia went on, "Anne is absurdly softhearted. And all the Bradfords take their responsibilities so seriously. I wonder Colonel Jim doesn't get to work and find you a husband as long as Chris has to keep you at the Manor until you get one."

"Perhaps," Beth said, forcing herself to speak through stiff lips, "you would like to wait for Nan. If you'll excuse me, I have an engagement."

As she opened the door into the hotel corridor, Julia said, "With an admirer? Then I suggest you bring him to the sticking point. Don't forget my advice. Marry someone and set both Anne and Chris free."

Beth rang the bell for the elevator, stepped inside and went down, unconscious of the admiring male glances that brushed over her. In her mind she could hear Chris's amused voice warning her, "Remember Julia." But this time it did not help.

She drank coffee and ate half a grapefruit and then, drawing her fur piece closer about her neck, went through the lobby to the street. Ordinarily, she would have been interested in the people who thronged the huge room, the smartly dressed women, a famous character actor, the faces of celebrities familiar to her because she had often seen their pictures in the newspapers, But today she was oblivious to everything but the turmoil in her own mind.

Who had left that note in her bedroom? How had he—or she—gotten into a locked room? Had her father been murdered? *Murdered!* Was she spoiling Nan's life, preventing her marriage? It's hard to wait, the colonel had said. Wait to be free of her?

Before she reached the staircase leading down to the Park Avenue street entrance she saw Craven, leaning against the wall, wearing a beautifully tailored suit of pale gray. He straightened up and came toward her, his face alight. He was an important-looking man, she thought vaguely. Something about him made one think that here was a captain of great enterprises.

"This is luck!" he exclaimed. "I have been standing here for the past ten minutes, debating whether I had the courage to present myself to Mrs. Bradford before luncheon. Where are you going? May I walk along or get you a taxi?"

"I—I don't really know where I am going," Beth admitted. "Just for a walk on Fifth Avenue to look in the shops until Nan returns."

"Then your time is free?" He took her silence for consent. "Wonderful! This is the reward of patience. In that smart little black number you are terrific. French, isn't it? I'll have every man who sees you madly jealous of me. I'll leave a note for Mrs. Bradford at the desk, shall I, so she'll know where you are?"

Beth nodded dumbly. She did not seem to be capable of speech. You've got to wake up, she scolded herself, to shake off this dazed feeling. You don't know what you are doing.

Craven was back in just a moment, his fair hair topping most of the men whom he passed, his colorless eyes gleaming with pleasure.

"Why not take my car?" he suggested, and led her to the elevator. They went down to a lower level of the hotel, where his car was brought from the garage. It was a long foreign two-seater, an eye-catching car, with a deep-throated rumble when he stepped on the accelerator.

Craven drove competently, as he seemed to do everything. He turned the car up Park Avenue, switched over to Fifth and threaded his way through the park and over to Riverside Drive.

Last night, Beth thought, I was driving through the park in a hansom cab with Chris. We saw that terrible accident and Chris held me in his arms, comforting me.

The Hudson River sparkled with pale blue light and the Palisades beyond were sheer drops of jagged rock. Craven drove slowly, not attempting to talk to her, and Beth was grateful to him. She leaned back, feeling the air crisp on her face, seeing the lovely slender line of the George Washington Bridge misty in the distance, the apartment buildings extending apparently forever, the soaring tower of the Rockefeller Church, the squat tomb of Grant.

The car, moving at greater speed than Beth realized, passed the complicated turns that led to the bridge itself and turned up the Henry Hudson Parkway. Beth realized that they were beyond the Cloisters, that they were out of Manhattan and headed north.

"Shouldn't we start back?" she asked.

"That is all taken care of," Craven assured her. "In the note I left for Mrs. Bradford I told her I was taking you for a drive and that you would not return for luncheon. Forgive me, I had no right, but a desperate man will snatch at a crumb of bread, and this drive is the very first crumb that has fallen to the lot of this starving man."

He managed to keep his tone so light that it did not disturb Beth, and in her bemused state she was glad to be riding, without effort or volition of her own, postponing the moment when she must decide what to do in order to free Anne. And always, hammering at her mind with a dull pain, were the words: Who killed your father and stole his formula? Because Chris himself had revealed accidentally to her that her father had been killed, and Chris himself was going to manufacture the formula. And the pain was more than Beth could bear.

The long foreign sports car had passed the first

toll station before Craven spoke. "Tell me what is wrong," he said, so quietly that his voice did not jar on her mood. "I love you, Beth. You must know that. I want to help you. I want you to marry me. I want you to be the happiest girl on earth and I believe I am the man who can make you so. I can't bear seeing you as unhappy as you are now. Try to share your your troubles with me. I am not your guardian, simply a man who wants, more than anything on earth, to take away your troubles and teach you what it is to be happy."

"That's—very kind of you."

"Kind!" Craven exploded.

Still dazed, Beth stared ahead at the road. Marry Mark Craven? Then her mind leaped into activity. The man was tremendously in earnest. She remembered Evelyn's warning and rejected it as the trick of a jealous woman. Mark Craven could not want her because of the formula. He was a wealthy man in his own right. He did not need the money. And she would be safe with him.

She pulled her furs closer around her.

"Cold?" Craven asked, quick to see the gesture. "Shall I put the top up?"

"No," she answered. For that would not warm her. The coldness was in her bones, a chill that ran down her spine. Marry Mark Craven? Then Nan would be free; she and Colonel Jim would not have to sacrifice their happiness on her account. Colonel Jim would no longer pace up and down, saying: It's hard to wait. She would not have to go on with this ghastly pretense with Chris, playing the game of a shadowy romance.

Who killed your father and stole his formula?

Craven began to speak quietly, and after a few moments she forced herself to listen to him. He told her of the home he would build for her, of the life she would lead, of the happiness she would give him, of his love for her. He did not attempt to touch her; his voice and manner were gentle.

"Chris would never give his consent," she said abruptly.

Craven laughed. "I am sure of that," he said grimly, "but after all, my beautiful, you are of age, you know. There is nothing he can do legally to stop you." After a pause, he said, "And why should he want to prevent you from marrying to suit yourself?"

I don't know why, Beth told herself, though she made no answer aloud. But I do know that Chris doesn't want me to see Mark Craven; he forbade me —forbade me!—to do anything for poor Mr. Smith. Oh, Chris, Chris!

Craven was apparently unaware of her tumult of mind. He kept his eyes on the road and his hands on the wheel of the powerful car. In a detached way Beth appreciated his restraint. She was grateful that he had made no attempt to touch her.

"Marry me," he said again, still not looking at her. "Marry me, Beth, and let me take care of you." His voice was slow, hypnotic. "Marry me."

"All—all right," she said shakily.

The car shot ahead as his foot pressed on the accelerator. "You will!" He brought the car under control, drew it to the side of the road, stopped, faced her at last. His burning eyes devoured her face but he was too wise to rush things. He caught her hands and kissed them, saw the yellow diamond gleaming on her left hand and drew it off.

He handed it to her with a laugh. "I'll replace this," he said.

Automatically, Beth dropped the ring into her handbag. She felt as though she were being swept around and around in a whirlpool.

Craven started the car again.

"Hadn't we better go back?" Beth asked.

"We're going to get married," Craven told her exultantly. He began to plan aloud, his voice jubilant.

"Now?" Beth was startled. "I haven't even—any clothes."

"We'll go to the Manor, where you can pack," he

said rapidly. "Then we'll take a plane to Maine and get married there."

The car rocketed along the parkway. It required all Craven's attention now, and Beth, her hands gripped together feverishly in her lap, wondered blankly, "What have I done? What am I doing?"

At length he pulled up in the circular entrance before the Manor. "Pack quickly," he told her. "You will need only one small bag. You can do all the shopping you like later on."

She went into the house. It was quiet, no voices anywhere. She stumbled up the stairs to her own room and packed a small bag, shaking so that she could not manage to fasten it without fumbling. She looked at the girl in the mirror, at wide shocked eyes and chalk-white face. Not much like a bride, she told herself.

Would she ever see this dear, familiar room again? For a long time she looked around her, saying good-by to it, then she turned and went out the door and down the stairs. She paused abruptly. Someone was in the study. Chris! Of course, he had come home.

She went down the stairs on tip-toe, started softly along the hallway to the door. The study door opened. It was not Chris who came out, it was Mark Craven.

"What were you doing in Chris's study?" she demanded.

He had been scowling when she first saw him; now the look changed. There was a triumphant light in his eyes when he seized her in his arms and kissed her with a passion which frightened her. It was the one touch needed to bring her to herself.

She pulled back, struggling to free herself from his arms. What horrible thing had she done? All at once she sensed something infinitely repulsive, something like a beast of prey, lurking behind his personality. She must have been mad to trust him. Her body seemed to flame with mortification.

"Let me go," she panted. "Let me go."

He laughed. "Never! My little wife."

"I can't marry you," Beth panted. "I can't. I was

crazy to think that I could." Seeing the change in his face, she implored him, "I know, I had no right to say that I would. But—something had happened; I was dazed, I didn't know what I was doing."

He bent over her deliberately, kissed her again.

"No! No!" she whispered.

He looked into her eyes and saw the repulsion, the horror she could not conceal, and knew that she had meant it, knew that he had lost her. Something moved behind his eyes and his arms tightened. "You are mine," he said, "and I intend to keep you."

She strangled back an impulse to scream. If she did, instinct warned her, she would never, never get away. She was awake now, prepared to fight, and the excitement of battle brought color back to her face, the light back to her eyes.

Unexpectedly, he caught her up in his arms and carried her out to the car. She clung to the door. "Let me go," she choked. "Let me go."

He flung himself in beside her, started the car with a roar and shot out of the driveway.

"Mark! Where are you taking me?"

He made no reply. The car was moving at sixty miles, at seventy, at eighty. She could not jump. Craven made no attempt to slow for the curves, it seemed to her that the car turned on two wheels. He passed other cars, swinging wildly back into line, avoiding oncoming vehicles with a sharp twist of his wrists. The thing was a nightmare. Beth closed her eyes. Opened them. She stole a glance at his profile, at the twitching line of a hard mouth, the flaring of his nostril. She shivered. He was cruel, ruthless.

They rocketed along an open stretch of road. "You can't kidnap me," she said at last. "That is a federal crime. There is a death sentence for it."

"Kidnaping," he said. His lips twitched in amusement. "This is not a kidnaping, my beautiful. It is an elopement."

"But—"

"You will have to marry me now," he said.

XV

Some time about the middle of the afternoon Craven turned the car onto an unused side road, got out and removed the key. Beth watched him go around to the back and unlock the trunk. An hour earlier, on a deserted strip of road, Craven had put up the top. She could blow the horn but there was no one on the road to hear her, no one at all. She could run but he could catch her in a matter of moments.

She fumbled in her handbag and pulled out a tiny engagement book and a pencil. She ripped out a page and wrote, *I am being kidnaped. The car license is AH789. Notify police and Christopher Bradford. Elizabeth Gilbert.* She folded it and then, realizing that no one would be apt to see a tiny scrap of paper, she reached up, unfastened a glittering gold pin she wore on the lapel of her black suit, and pinned it through the note. Sooner or later, there would be an opportunity to leave the note and the pin where they could be seen.

Don't get in a panic, she told herself. Keep your head. You will be lost if you let yourself be frightened. Watch for a chance to get away. He'll have to stop for gas and oil eventually. Something will happen. Something has to happen.

In a few moments Craven slammed down the top of the luggage compartment and came around the side of the car, his arms laden with packages which he put on the seat between them.

"Sandwiches and coffee," he said briefly. "Help yourself. If you would prefer something fancier, blame yourself. I'd like to take you to a nice restaurant but I don't trust you."

Beth was about to refuse the food indignantly when

it occurred to her that she would accomplish nothing by losing strength. She might need all she had later on, if she were to escape. She opened the paper bag beside her, took out a sandwich and a carton of coffee. The coffee was scalding hot and she felt better after drinking it, more alert, better able to cope with the situation.

"Where are you taking me?" she asked at length.

He made no reply. They must be well into Massachusetts by now, Beth thought. She no longer knew the roads though she watched carefully, checking the road numbers and memorizing the turns Craven made. They passed comparatively few cars.

It was when the gray coupé passed them that Beth straightened up in her seat. Then, fearing that Craven would notice her interest, she forced herself to lean back, eyes half closed as though she were falling asleep. But her mind was working furiously. That gray coupé with the battered fender. She had seen it earlier in the afternoon. Then, later on, Craven had overtaken and passed him.

Perhaps someone was following them! If there were only some way of conveying a message. A little later, she saw the gray coupé ahead of them again. It was drawn up at the side of the road and the driver had the hood up and seemed to be tinkering with the motor. As they approached, she turned her head toward Craven, looking intently out of his side of the car, to distract his attention from the gray coupé. Craven, noticing her sudden interest, let his eyes follow hers. She looked back quickly. The driver had straightened up, a heavy man with massive shoulders and a bald head.

Surely, Beth thought, that was the man who had been lurking in the garden at the Manor! Then it was no accident that the gray coupé kept reappearing along the road. The man was following them. But was he following Craven or Beth? Could this be the man who had shadowed her in Europe? If that was the case, then there was nothing to be hoped from him; this was another enemy, or an accomplice of Craven's.

Craven had begun to slow down. Had he seen the man in the gray coupé? No, he was watching the road signs intently. Now he was turning off the highway onto a narrow winding lane. There had been no road work done for some time, and he reduced his speed almost to a crawl as they jolted over the ruts. The sun had gone behind massed clouds and the lane was dark.

There were no houses in sight; there had been no houses for a long time, Beth realized. No one would hear her if she were to shout for help. A rabbit scuttled across the road and vanished into the woods with a dry rustle of dead leaves. The lane had faded to a dim track, crossed by a second, even fainter trail, and Craven stopped the car, looking uncertainly along the two roads, if they could be called roads. It was still, so breathlessly still that Beth caught herself holding her breath. There was no sound of any car behind them. The gray coupé must have gone on its way.

The gray clouds were turning black and massing heavily now; it was very dark in the woods. Craven switched on the lights and turned onto the fainter of the two paths, creeping along the lane, which was so narrow that the branches brushed against the sides of the car. At length he came into the little clearing in which there was a small shack, and he gave a grunt of satisfaction, shut off the motor and got out.

He came around to Beth's door and opened it. "Get out," he said briefly.

She climbed out stiffly—there was nothing else to do —and gathered her forces for flight. Something of her intention must have shown in her face, for he laughed softly.

"Scream if you want to," he jeered, "and you might attract the attention of some late birds flying south. Run—but you can't get away from me in those high heels and in the dark."

It was so obviously true that Beth stood stock-still. Craven, ignoring her, went around to the trunk, where he took out several large paper bags and carried them into the shack. Beth drifted as far back of the car as she dared and put down the pin and the note in the middle of the lane. There was small hope that anyone would come this way, less hope that the gleaming jewel would be seen, and always the grim chance that someone would take the pin and ignore the plea for help. But it was the best she could do.

Craven came out of the shack, a big flashlight in his hand. "All right," he said briefly. "You'd better get inside."

Beth hesitated for a moment, taking a last despairing look around her in search of help. Then there was a long rumble of thunder and a distant flash of lightning. Craven's hand fastened around her arm and he dragged her inside the shack.

It was a two-room dwelling, with a rough, unpainted table in the middle of the main room, on which stood some unwashed dishes. There were a wood range grown rusty from neglect, a sink with a pump attached, and several kitchen chairs. Beyond was a bedroom containing a chest of drawers, a broken chair and a small cot.

The place had the musty smell of the long unused, and over everything was a coating of dust and grime. It was filthy. Mice scuttled through the walls, spider webs festooned the ceiling. The floor was not merely dirty, there was a film of grease over it.

"Not the Waldorf," Craven admitted, watching her expression in amusement, "but it's your home for the time being so you might as well settle down and stop hovering there at the door. You aren't going anywhere for a long, long time."

He set a big flashlight on the table until he could pull some candles out of one of the paper bags. He lighted them and stuck them into two chipped dirty saucers.

"I'll start a fire in the stove and pump up some water," he said as she began to shiver from the cold, dead air in the place. "You may as well be useful as well as ornamental and cook our supper. You'll find food for several days in those packages."

He switched off the flashlight, and the two candles made dim flickering pools of light that only accentuated the darkness of the little shack, through whose grimy, spider-web-covered window panes no light trickled. Even if there was any more light. For the storm had shut off the last of the daylight.

The roll of thunder was almost constant now, and lightning flashed and crackled more and more loudly, closer and closer.

Craven shook down the stove and built a fire, and in spite of herself Beth was grateful for the warmth. A crash of thunder and a blinding blaze of lightning struck almost simultaneously, and Craven, who had been pumping water vigorously, started.

"That was close!" he exclaimed.

I hope it hits this shack, Beth thought passionately. Better to die like that—no, I'm ashamed of you, Beth Gilbert. You can't give up so easily. Remember your American history: We have not yet begun to fight.

What do I do first? Better put Mark Craven off guard. If he believes I have given up all hope of escape he will be less apt to watch me so closely. It cheered her to discover that Craven was more upset by the storm than she was. Twice, as lightning flashed, he mopped his head with a shaking hand.

The room had begun to lose its chill and she removed her hat and gloves and furs, leaving them where she could snatch them up in a hurry, her handbag lying on top. How much money did she have with her, in case she could get away, in case she could reach a telephone or the police? She dared not look to see.

"Well," she said, with a challenge in her voice, her shoulders back, chin up, a sparkle in her eyes, "I'll see what I can do about supper."

She opened the paper bags, took out the food and looked it over. She smothered a giggle when she saw that Craven had bought canned lobster Newburg, mushroom caps, French peas. This was kidnaping de luxe. She opened the cans, washed some pans and, while the food was heating, she scrubbed the table vigorously, washed the dishes and reset the table.

Craven left the window where he had been peering anxiously into the storm and hovered around, a glint of admiration in his eyes.

"You know, Beth," he said, "we could go places together. I take off my hat to you. There's not a girl in a million who would be such a good sport. I expected you to be dissolved in tears."

I hope you'll never guess how close I am to it, Beth thought. She managed a laugh.

"We have to eat," she said lightly. "Anyhow, I'm not afraid, because you won't get away with this, Mark Craven."

"Is that what you think?" he mocked her.

"I know," she said, with such assurance that for a moment he was shaken. "Dinner is on the table, such as it is."

They sat facing each other across the flickering candlelight in the little shack. The situation was so improbable that Beth found it difficult to believe that she was here, Mark Craven's prisoner.

For a moment the storm semed to diminish and then there was a new sound, a deluge of rain beating on the tin roof, so loud that it was deafening.

"Why are you doing this?" Beth said, almost shouting in order to be heard above the tumult of the storm.

Mark smiled at her, his colorless eyes like muddy water in a pool churned up by rain. "If you wouldn't marry me willingly, I had to find some way of—persuading you."

"You're behind the times," Beth said coolly. "Girls are no longer impressed by caveman tactics, or haven't you heard?"

"Being married to you will be a most interesting experience," he laughed.

"But why? You aren't in love with me."

"Curiously enough, I am," Craven said. "I was bowled over the first time I met you. And you have everything I want in a wife: you are beautiful, you are courageous, and you are—rich."

Beth laughed outright. "Rich? I have nothing but an allowance from Chris that barely keeps me in clothes and money for traveling."

"Rich, I meant," Craven explained, "when your father's formula is manufactured. Beth"—he leaned forward—"be a sensible girl. Don't force me to use—what you call caveman tactics. And make no mistake, I'll do it if necessary. Say the word and we'll go on to an airport as soon as this storm is over—the flights will probably be canceled anyhow for the next hour or so—and fly to Maine to be married. Believe me, we could be happy together. And I know more about putting that formula on the market than anyone else. I can do more for you with it than Christopher Bradford can any day."

"But I don't have the formula," she protested. "I have never seen it in all my life. My father never discussed it with me."

"I know you haven't got it," he said impatiently. "Christopher Bradford has it, has had it ever since your father was knocked down and robbed in the Bradford driveway. But legally it belongs to you. Without your permission he can't do anything with it."

Christopher Bradford has it. Craven spoke with such conviction that Beth could not doubt him. Anyhow, Chris himself had made public the fact that he was going to manufacture it. Then how had he obtained it? How?

Behind Craven's head the window was black, streaked with heavy rivulets of rain. And then, against the blackness, something moved.

Beth's heart leaped in her throat. Carefully she forced herself to look away from the window, to let her eyes rest on Craven's face.

"Some more lobster?" she asked with difficulty. Anything to prevent Craven from turning around.

Then she stifled a scream.

"What is it?" Craven asked sharply.

"A mouse," she said, a touch of hysteria in her voice.

Craven laughed. "And I thought you were courageous! It's a funny thing, you haven't got at all fussed by being eloped with but the sight of a mouse—" He chuckled to himself.

"Silly of me," Beth admitted. Of course there wasn't a mouse. What had startled her was a white, formless blob pressed against the window. Her heart seemed to leap into her throat, it was choking her. The blob was a nose pressed flat against the pane.

She reached for his empty plate and got to her feet.

"What a domestic little wife I am going to have," Craven said laughing.

The white blob was gone but out in the rain there were eyes watching their every move. Beth brought the refilled plate back from the stove. The knob of the door was turning soundlessly, or at any rate the sound was covered by the storm. She stood beside Craven while she handed him the plate so that he could not see the turning knob.

Her nearness inflamed Craven and he turned suddenly, his hands reaching for her. Then, so abruptly that she started, spilling the food onto the table, the door was flung open and crashed back against the wall, sending a spray of rain into the room. A man stood there in a streaming raincoat, a man with massive shoulders and a gleaming bald head. A man with a revolver in his hand.

And the man was Stone.

Craven's chair fell over with a crash. "Who the hell are you?" he demanded.

The revolver was pointed at Craven and the hand that held it was as steady as a rock.

"Get your coat, miss," Stone said without moving his eyes from Craven's face.

"You can't get away with this," Craven blustered. "Beth, stay where you are."

She backed toward the door, reached blindly for her coat and furs, pulled on her hat, clutched handbag and gloves.

"I'm ready," she said breathlessly.

"Very good, miss," the butler-detective said stolidly. "You go first. I'll cover for you. It's a—"

"I know," she said. "It's a gray coupé. I thought you were following us."

Craven cursed softly and horribly.

She took one last look at the big fair man standing at bay in the candlelit shack, at the detective with his gleaming bald head, his dripping raincoat, his steady revolver. Then she plunged out into the torrential rain, half blinded, almost breathless. She ran past the dark mass of Craven's two-seater, toward the headlights of a car. She got in. The key was there, she turned it, started the motor. In a moment Stone came running out and she slid over into the other seat while he got under the wheel.

"Good work," he said as he put the car in gear.

"Can we get away?" she asked. "He has a more powerful car."

"This motor has been souped up," he told her. "You'd be surprised at what it can do. Anyhow, it will take Craven a couple of hours to fix that motor after what I've done to it." He chuckled. "And is he going to get wet doing it! I'd like to see his face when he tries to start that car."

"I never was so glad to see anyone in all my life," Beth told him.

Something dropped in her lap, the gold pin fastened to the slip of paper.

"Found your note," he said briefly. "You did some nice thinking there. But I didn't need it. I've been right behind you ever since you and Craven left the hotel. For a while there I thought my hunch was all wrong and you were in this with Craven, until I saw him force you into the car. And when I passed you a coupla times and got a good look at your face I knew you weren't taking that ride for pleasure."

"Pleasure!" Beth exclaimed feelingly. "I've never been more frightened in all my life."

The car skidded sickeningly over the mud, the road was barely visible through the headlights.

"There should be a state police station somewhere," she suggested. "There—there it is!"

To her surprise, the car instead of slowing down began to move faster now that it had reached a highway and a good road.

"Mr. Stone! The police."

"All in good time, Miss Gilbert," he said phlegmatically.

A chill of doubt went over Beth. "But—what—where are you going?" she asked.

"I'm going to expose your father's murderer," he said grimly. "This time there is to be no slip-up. When I've caught him and made him confess I'll call the police. Not before."

"Do you know who it is?" she asked, her voice barely above a whisper.

"Yes, at last I know."

"Who?"

"Christopher Bradford."

XVI

At one-thirty that afternoon, Anne Bradford stopped at the desk in the lobby going up to her suite.

"Any messages?" she asked.

The clerk handed her a list of telephone calls and an envelope addressed in unknown handwriting. She looked at the list of calls: Evelyn Furnas, Mrs. Julia Seagreave. She ripped open the envelope as she stepped into the elevator. As she read it the color drained out of her charming face.

"Oh, no!" she moaned. "Oh, no."

The elevator girl, trim in her smart uniform, turned quickly. "Is madam ill?"

Anne pulled herself together with a gallant effort and summoned up a smile. "Thank you, I am just a little—fatigued."

She got off at her floor and started blindly down the corridor. Then she stopped and went back to the floor desk, where an elderly woman was sitting.

"Do you know," she asked, "whether anyone has called since I went out this morning?"

The clerk looked down at her day book. "A Mrs. Seagreave called. She said she would return at one-thirty."

I simply can't cope with Julia now, Anne thought frantically. What made Beth do such an insane thing? I thought she loved Chris. Oh, my poor Chris, how am I going to tell him? He'll be heartbroken. If she had done it some other way, told us she cared for Mark Craven—but she didn't, Ann thought clearly. I know Beth. She doesn't care two straws for the man. And it isn't his money; she would never marry a man for that. Then why—

Her thoughts whirled. Steadied.

"What's that?" she asked sharply.

The clerk looked curiously at the white-faced woman who seemed to be in a daze.

"The night clerk," she repeated, "wasn't sure, but the lady said she was expected at your suite, and it was such an odd hour—"

"I'm sorry," Anne said. "I was wool-gathering. Will you please repeat that?"

"That night clerk said a young lady, tall, blond, blue-eyed, in a mink coat, came up at two o'clock this morning. When she was asked where she was going she said your suite and you were expecting her. She stayed only a few moments or the clerk would have checked with you. I hope that was all right."

That description could fit only Evelyn Furnas. What on earth had she been doing at that time of night? She had not aroused Anne. Could she have gone to Beth's room? Could she have been responsible for Beth's elopement?

"It's all right," Anne said aloud to the clerk and went on down the corridor and around a corner to her own suite. It was empty. No sign of Beth. No note. No—on the floor there was a crumpled envelope. Perhaps Beth had left a note and forgotten it in her excitement. Anne pulled out a sheet of paper on which had been pasted letters cut from a newspaper: WHO KILLED YOUR FATHER AND STOLE HIS FORMULA?

Evelyn! Anne thought instantly. That is what she was doing. She left that for Beth. She wanted to make her distrust Chris. Of all the infamous—

There was a tap at the door. Word from Beth? Beth herself come back on thinking things over? "Come in," she called eagerly.

Julia Seagreave swept in. "At last," she exclaimed. "I thought I'd *never* find you. Beth said you planned to lunch at one-thirty. I'll join you." She looked more closely at Anne's white face. "Anne, you look ghastly. Poor dear, you needn't explain. I know all about it."

"You know?" Anne stammered.

"Yes, I know you are sacrificing yourself and postponing your marriage to the dear colonel because you can't leave Beth at the Manor. I told her so this morning. Of all the selfish—"

"You told her what, Julia?" Anne Bradford's voice held a note that startled the widow.

"Why, that if she had any decency at all she would get married and free you and Chris from your responsibility."

"You have done a terrible thing, Julia. A terrible thing. And it may be too late to undo it."

"Well, I must say, of all the preposterous—"

Anne did not listen to her sputtering protests. She picked up the telephone and called the Manor.

Before noon that same day Christopher Bradford and Colonel Haswell got out of a taxi in front of the Manor and hastened up the steps. Just as they were about to enter the house there was the roar of a motor and a gay hail. Ted had drawn up behind them in his new car.

"For the love of Mike, Chris," he exclaimed, "can't you take off a single day for fun without having to come rushing back? This place can survive for twenty-four hours without you."

"Ted, come on in and tell me again about finding Rose in my study."

The boy's eyes widened. "So that's it," he said. He followed the two men into Chris's study. Chris went at once to the safe. There was a grim smile on his face when he saw that the picture which hung in front of it was slightly askew.

"Someone has been tampering with it, all right," he told Haswell. He opened the safe and checked quickly through the papers. "Nothing taken, though I had several hundred dollars in cash for staff salaries. Still here. But everything has been moved around. Well, that's that."

He swung the safe door shut, twirled the dial, and turned to Ted. "Now then, let's have it."

"Well, there's really nothing much to tell. Gosh, do

you mean to say that we had a robbery here last night and I missed all the excitement?" The boy sounded so aggrieved that, in spite of his anxiety, Colonel Jim smiled.

"Go on, Ted," Chris prodded him.

"Believe it or not, I was studying. I needed a dictionary and I was too lazy to go up to my room for it so I came in here. I knew you had dictionaries in half a dozen languages on your desk. There was Rose sound asleep on the floor in front of the fireplace. I never was so surprised. I spoke to her several times and then I shook her. She came up in a single spring, crying out, 'Don't do it! Don't do it!' Then she seemed to be wide awake, and looked as surprised as I felt when she saw who I was. That was when she said something about walking in her sleep. But she was so darned excited that I thought she was out of her head and I went to ask Smithy what he thought I'd better do. Only Smithy—wasn't there."

"Where is Rose now?"

"I telephoned Mummy to ask her what I'd better do but she was in New York—"

"Mummy in New York on a weekday?" Chris exclaimed in surprise. "I never knew her to do that before."

"I know," Ted agreed. "It never happened before. The whole thing seemed to be a conspiracy to make me use my own head. Anyhow, just to be on the safe side, I telephoned to Dr. Russell and he came over, said Rose had a rapid pulse and was highly nervous, and he gave her a sedative. I saw her this morning, as I told you over the phone. She was arranging the buffet for breakfast. I told her to take it easy. I asked Katie about her just before I went out for a ride—and oh, Chris, does that buggy move!—and Katie said Rose had gone back to her room and she was sleeping like a baby."

"Probably still under the influence of the sedative. We won't wake her now," Chris decided. "Better let her sleep it off and then we'll be able to get more sense out of her. But the time has come for that girl to talk. Now we'll take a look at Smith's room."

"Look, Chris," Ted protested. "I don't know what any of this is about but you're all wrong about Smithy. You've been down on him for a long time, I could see that, only—only he's a swell guy. If you think for a moment he would rob your old safe, you're off your head."

Chris's hand rested on his younger brother's shoulder. How loyal the boy was! "Take it easy," he said gently. "You can trust us. Colonel Jim and I won't do anything unfair; we'll give the man every chance. But your friend Smith has a lot of explaining to do, Ted. If he's in the clear, so much the better."

"But you don't think he is?" The boy's eyes were anxious.

"I'm afraid not."

"I'm going with you," Ted declared. "I know you two mean well but—there's just no one on Smith's side but me."

"Come along," Chris agreed.

They tapped on the tutor's door, and when there was no answer they went in. The room was empty. For a moment Chris stood in the doorway looking over the room. The bed had been turned down but it had not been slept in. There were no signs of disorder. Smith had not taken his clothes with him. His shaving equipment and toothbrush were in their proper place, no clothing seemed to be missing.

"What was he wearing yesterday, do you know?" Chris asked.

"Navy blue slacks and a navy blue pullover," Ted replied.

Chris picked up a pullover that was lying on a chair. "This one?"

Ted nodded. "That's the only one he had. I don't suppose you've noticed, the way I did, that he doesn't have many clothes. I suspect he's awfully hard up. Say, that's queer!" He opened the closet door and ran an eye over the hangers. "Smithy didn't take a topcoat, not even a jacket. Why, the man hasn't on any sort of coat and it was darned cold last night, down to twenty-eight." He looked at Chris's face and his eye widened. "What do you think has happened to him, Chris?"

"I don't like this," Chris said slowly.

The tutor's desk was near the windows. His papers were blowing over the floor in the breeze from the window that opened on the balcony. "He would never have gone off and left them like that," he declared.

"Then something *has* happened to him," Ted insisted.

"Could be."

They returned to Chris's study, where Colonel Haswell called his housekeeper.

"Mrs. Altman? Any sign of Stone yet? . . . " He turned to Chris. "He hasn't returned. What about it?"

"We can't wait any longer," Chris declared. "We need action and we need it fast."

"Mrs. Altman," the colonel said, "I am putting in a call for the police. If they should come to the house before I return, answer any questions they may ask."

But it was Christopher Bradford who called the police. He talked for a long time. At last he set down the telephone and exhaled a long sigh. "Well, we've started things happening, Colonel Jim. I hope we've done the right thing."

Ted was very white. "So that's it," he said. "So that's it. That is why Beth's room was torn apart. It is the Gilbert formula someone is looking for. But if you don't have it, Chris, who does?"

"The man who killed Beth's father," Chris told him grimly.

"And that is?"

"I don't know," Chris said with a groan. "But it must be either Stone or Smith."

"Not Smithy," Ted declared hotly. "I tell you, Chris, I know the guy and I—I like him."

"I hope not," Chris declared. "Because you believe in him."

Ted got up restlessly. "What do we do now?"

"We wait," Chris said. "Until we can hear from the police there is nothing to do. The matter is in their hands now."

"You mean that with a countrywide search out for Smithy we are just going to sit here?" the boy protested hotly.

The telephone pealed and Chris answered it. "Yes? . . . Long distance? I'll hold the line. . . . Yes? That you, Mother? . . . I can't hear you. Don't cry, dear. . . . *What!* Beth's gone! Eloped? . . . Read the message again." Chris reached for paper and pencil and scrawled down words at his mother's dictation. "Have I got this straight? *Dear Mrs. Bradford, Beth and I have discovered that we love each other, and since we are both of age we are taking matters into our own hands. We are going to be married today. Beth will get in touch with you after our honeymoon. She sends you her regards. Mark Craven.* . . . No, there is nothing you can do in New York, Mother. You'd probably be happier if you return here so you can be with us. Beth won't be in New York anyhow. It takes three days there. . . . What! Bring her clothes with you? Do you mean that Beth went off without taking anything with her? . . . No. No. I was just surprised. Nothing for you to worry about. Don't bother with the car as long as Beth isn't there to drive it. Take the train."

Chris put down the telephone and dropped his head into his hands with a groan. There was no sound in the room but the crackling of the fire in the grate and the ticking of the clock on the mantel. When he raised his head at last, Ted and Colonel Jim were shocked by the ravaged face he revealed.

"You heard that," he said unsteadily. "Craven's got Beth."

"I wouldn't have believed she would want to marry

him," Ted said in bewilderment. So much was happening that he could not cope with it. "She never seemed to like him very much. And to run away like that without telling you—"

"She didn't run away," Chris said through white lips. "That message was all Craven. Beth would never send her 'regards' to Mother. She would not go off, leaving her clothes unpacked, taking nothing with her. She wouldn't—marry Craven—without telling us."

"You love her, don't you?" Ted said.

"Yes, I love her." Chris got up blindly. "What shall I do, Colonel Jim? If I call the police I'll drag Beth's name into this. If I don't—"

"Do you mean," Ted gasped, his face turning from red to dead white, "that you think she was taken against her will?"

"It must be that way. I tell you—I believe in Beth."

"So do I," Ted growled. "Chris, can't we do something—look for her ourselves—"

"But where—where?"

"Then we've got to tell the police. There is no other possibility."

"But it can't be a coincidence," Colonel Haswell said thoughtfully, "that everything is happening at once: the disappearance of Stone and Smith, Rose's peculiar behavior, the kidnapping of Beth by Craven."

"Coincidence!" Chris snapped. "Of course not. And I precipitated everything by the fool announcement that I was going to manufacture the Gilbert formula. I ought to have my head examined."

"But what," Ted demanded, utterly confused, "is the connection between Smithy and all these other things?"

"I don't know," Chris admitted. "But there is something—"

He stood at the Dutch door with his back to them, his hands clenching and unclenching in his pockets. Somewhere—but where? Where?—Beth was in Mark Craven's power. "My time will come," Craven had said with his queer smile. Well, it had come all right. Where had he taken her? What was he doing with her? Why had he done it? Did he really believe that she would marry him, that he could force her into marriage? Would he—hurt her?

He bit back a groan of rage and horror as he thought of the girl's wide beautiful eyes, her brilliant smile, her gay companionship, her sweetness. No one could hurt her. Surely, no one could hurt anything so lovely.

If only he had told her the whole story in the first place! Would it have made any difference? But how could it? And he had wanted to spare her the knowledge that her father was murdered; he had not wanted her to know that she herself was in danger. And, like a fool, he had been so sure that he could protect her.

Arrogant, blind idiot, he told himself in bitterness and anguish and regret. If you had told Beth the whole story, you might have prevented this. You know how gallant she is; she could face anything. Under all her softness and gentleness and sweetness there is the tempered steel of a strong will and real character.

As though she were already dead, he thought of her in the past. He remembered his sharpness to her of late, a result of his anxiety about her; the fact that he had been, from her standpoint, unreasonable and he could not explain why. He remembered how he had snapped at her when she had slipped her hand under his arm. He groaned aloud.

"Chris!" Colonel Haswell said authoritatively. "You are torturing yourself. Worry won't accomplish anything. We've got to call the police."

Chris took a long breath and turned around. His face was chalk-white, his eyes burning. He took a step toward the telephone on the desk and stopped as the door of the study was flung open so hard it banged against the wall. Rose came racing into the room.

Her uniform was rumpled, her shoes muddy; a tweed coat hung over her shoulders. There was a smear of blood on the hem of her white skirt.

"Mr. Chris!" she cried. "Mr. Chris!"

"Oh, no," Ted muttered. "I can't stand much more. The girl's gone nuts."

"What is it, Rose?"

"It's Mr. Smith," she panted. She began to cry wildly, hysterically. "It's Mr. Smith. He's lying in the underbrush at the edge of the woods. Oh, Mr. Chris, someone killed him. He's dead. He's dead!"

XVII

"That's not true," Beth said clearly. "Christopher Bradford did not kill my father, Mr. Stone."

For a moment the butler-detective made no reply. The fury of the storm made driving almost impossible. It took muscular strength to keep the car on the road against the fierce onslaughts of wind. The torrential rain fell like a blinding curtain in front of the headlights so that it was difficult to see the road more than a car's length ahead.

Stone turned on the heater and leaned forward to open the glove compartment. He groped for a moment and then slid a toupee over his bald head.

"Why do you wear that?" Beth asked.

Stone laughed and suddenly he seemed more human than before. "No one wants a bald butler," he said. "Anyhow, on a night like this it is warmer."

As the car gradually lost its chill Beth stopped shaking.

"Feeling better now?" Stone asked.

"Much better."

"Then I want to talk to you, Miss Gilbert. I'm going to lay the facts before you. See what you make of them. You have a level head and I think you were fond of your father."

"Fond," Beth choked.

"So you will be able to have some detachment about the Bradfords. This is the story. Your father developed a formula for plastics that would have made him many times a millionaire. He worked secretly with the help of a single assistant, a man named Larry Sergent. There were, as is usual in such cases, a number of disappointments before the formula was finally satisfactory. Then your father discovered that he could

170

not handle the financing of his new product by himself, that it would require a lot of capital and knowhow on the part of someone who knew manufacturing and marketing as well as he knew chemistry.

"Mr. Gilbert did not confide in anyone. Through channels never revealed to a soul he made contact with a man who was interested and who was willing to gamble on the formula, to put up the money and go into partnership.

"Now this is what happened, Miss Gilbert. Your father was a shrewd man. He knew that what he had was worth a fortune and he was wise enough not to be blindly trusting. He left his laboratory, telling his assistant that he was going to call upon this would-be partner and discuss arrangements. But he did not take a chance. What he had with him was not the final formula, but a substitute. And where did he go to see the new partner? *To the Manor!*"

"But—but," Beth gasped— "He only stopped to call on Mr. Bradford. He was to meet the partner in New York."

"How do you know that?" Stone asked sharply.

"Chris said so."

"Yes," Stone said slowly, "Bradford said so. But has he ever been able to substantiate that story? Has anyone ever heard of that elusive partner since then?"

Beth was silent.

"And why, Miss Gilbert, if your father trusted Bradford so completely as he seemed to do, didn't he have the real formula with him?"

"How do you know he didn't have the real formula?" Beth asked.

"Because," Stone said coolly, "I know now where the real formula is." He went on before she could speak. "The night your father came to the Manor he was knocked down and robbed, and he died in the driveway. He never left the place. Coincidence? No, Miss Gilbert, he was murdered in cold blood."

"No one ever told me that," Beth whispered.

"Strange, isn't it?" Stone said.

"But not Chris," Beth said fiercely. "I know him. He

couldn't do it, he simply couldn't. And if it was for the formula, for money—you don't know what he is like. He isn't—greedy. He could easily make more money than he does if he wanted to be hard on his tenants. I tell you, I know."

The detective made no reply and Beth looked unseeingly at the ribbons of rain slanting across the road. "It could be the missing assistant," she said. "Don't you see how logical that would be? After all, Larry Sergent knew better than anyone else the value of that formula and he vanished on the same night. Or —or the partner."

"I've told you who I think the partner was," Stone reminded her.

"There's another thing," Beth went on. "Someone followed me in Europe and ransacked my luggage over and over. Someone searched my room the night I returned to the Manor."

"I followed you in Europe," Stone replied, "and I searched your luggage."

"You!"

"For a long time," he said, "I was—misled—about where the formula was. I thought your father might have left it with you. It was not until I returned here, a month before you did, that I learned where it really was and got the true facts about the situation. When I saw the whole picture, I knew I had been on the wrong track, but I stayed on the case to right a great wrong."

"Why were you following Mark Craven and me?" Beth asked. "Did you still think I—"

"I was curious," Stone admitted. "I couldn't figure out where he entered the picture and what he was after."

"He wants control of the formula," Beth told him. "And he hoped to get it by forcing me to marry him. Is he—could Mark Craven be the missing assistant, Larry Sergent?"

"No," Stone said, "I think he's just a guy who wants money so badly he would go to any lengths to get it. He's not really a part of the picture at all."

"At least—I'm grateful that you followed me today."

Stone nodded. "Things were bound to break sooner or later," he said.

"Mr. Stone, did you leave a—a message—in my hotel room?"

"No, I've been trying to keep out of sight, though there wasn't much chance of Craven recognizing me. He's only called a couple of times at Colonel Haswell's house and people don't usually pay much attention to servants."

"Why were you searching the pockets of Mark Craven's overcoat that night when I found you?"

"Just thought something of interest might turn up."

The rain was falling more lightly now and the wind had died down. The rain ceased altogether and Stone stopped the windshield wipers. He drove slowly. At length the sky began to lighten. Dawn broke. A gray morning it seemed at first. Stone switched off the lights. Then a patch of blue sky appeared and the sun caught the tops of the trees. Another day had come.

What will it bring with it, Beth wondered? The discovery of her father's murderer? An end to the mystery that had dogged her steps for months? Chris —no, she cried, deep in her heart. I believe in him. Whatever happens, I believe in him. Chris could not be dishonorable. He could not. Oh, Chris, darling, I love you so much!

The early morning hush was broken by the wail of a siren, rising and falling. It swelled, came nearer, a car rocked down the road. Now it slowed, the siren fading, and drew alongside the coupé.

Stone stopped his car and turned around. "What's wrong, officer? I didn't think I was speeding."

"Is your name Stone?"

"Yes."

"Who's the lady?"

"Miss Elizabeth Gilbert."

"Gilbert!" He called to the driver of the radio car. "Well, what do you know? We've got the girl to℮

only she's with the wrong man!" He turned back. "All right, Stone," he said crisply, "you get into that radio car; I'll drive yours. We're going places."

"Just a moment," Stone said, feeling for his wallet.

"Out," the officer said curtly. Stone, without a word, only a slight shrug of his shoulders, climbed out from under the wheel and got into the radio car, which shot off.

The officer took his place.

"Where are you taking me?" Beth asked. It occurred to her that this was the third man of whom she had asked that same question within the past twenty-four hours.

"Home," he said briefly.

Rose wheeled and raced out of the study, followed by the three men. But when it was clear in what direction they should look, Ted outdistanced the others. By the time Chris had reached his side, Ted was kneeling beside the man who lay sprawled on the ground in the underbrush, his broken glasses lying beside him, his face battered, eyes closed, color so ghastly that, for a moment, Chris shared Rose's belief that the tutor was dead.

Gently, he moved Ted to one side and took the man's wrist between his fingers. There seemed to be no pulse—yes, there was a feeble, irregular beat. He looked up.

"Smith is alive."

Rose gave a stifled cry.

"Get that folding cot from the garage, Ted. If we are careful we can lift him on that. We must be careful in moving him in case there is any injury to the spine." His sure fingers gently probed the unconscious man's head and he gave a sharp exclamation. "Someone struck a terrific blow. The skin is broken and there's a lot of dried blood on his hair. There's a lump the size of an egg but I don't know what other damage. Rose," he said to the weeping maid, "run inside and telephone to Dr. Russell. If he's not in his office, ask his nurse to trace him. This is an emergency."

Without a word the girl was running wildly across the lawn.

Colonel Haswell looked down at the face of the unconscious man.

"Do you think he'll live?"

"I don't know," Chris said. "His heartbeat is very faint and irregular and that blow on his head was meant to be for keeps. There may be an injury to the brain. Can't tell until the doctor comes."

Ted ran across the lawn carrying the folding cot, opened it rapidly. Together the three men lifted the injured tutor gently onto the cot, moving him as little as possible. Chris and Haswell carried the cot and Ted walked beside it, his anxious eyes on the unmoving man.

Rose held the door open and followed them up to Smith's room. When they had settled him on the bed Chris said, "Better not undress him now. We'll disturb him as little as possible until the doctor comes."

"He was just leaving on his rounds," Rose said in a whisper as though afraid she would wake Smith. "He's coming at once."

In a few moments they heard the screaming of brakes as a car was brought to a halt, the slam of a door, and Rose ran down the stairs to bring up the doctor.

While they waited for him to make his examination they went down to the drawing room.

"Come in, Rose," Chris said as she was about to slip away.

"I thought," she said, "the doctor might want something."

"He'll let us know if he does." He held open the door and the maid reluctantly came inside and stood twisting her coat sleeve, brushing her disheveled hair back with a muddy hand.

"How did you happen to find Mr. Smith?" Chris asked.

"I was—the doctor gave me some sleeping medicine last night. I had never taken any before and it made be groggy. When I woke up I thought I'd go out for some air to help me feel more awake, less dopey. I was just—walking down one of the garden paths—and looking toward the woods. I saw something white. It looked like a towel that had blown off the lines into the bushes; that happens sometimes. Then I saw it was a man's white shirt. He was lying in the bushes almost on his face. I saw the blood on his hair. I—turned him over. When I recognized Mr. Smith I came to you."

"Why did you fall asleep in front of the fireplace in my study last night, Rose?"

"I told Mr. Ted—I walk in my sleep."

"I know that is what you told him. But why did you do it? I want the truth."

She looked around in relief, grateful for the interruption, as the doctor came down the stairs.

"He's had a bad blow over the head," Dr. Russell said. "Concussion. He's been exposed to the night air and thinly clad. It looks to me as though he was injured some hours ago, perhaps as early as yesterday morning. He's in a state of shock and in danger of pneumonia. He'll probably be unconscious for hours. I wish I could get him into a hospital bed but the local hospital is filled to the rafters—why on earth don't more people leave money for hospitals?—and I don't think he should be moved to a more distant place. I'll try at least to get you a nurse but it may take some hours."

"I'll nurse him," Rose offered quickly. "I've studied first aid and I did home nursing a few years ago. I may have forgotten some things but I can carry out orders and I'll be careful."

The doctor studied her. "Good girl," he said in approval. "You ought to be in bed yourself but I think you'll handle this all right."

"I really will, Doctor; you can trust me," Rose said quietly.

"Then come along and I'll give you your orders. Let me know, of course, if there is any change, but I don't expect any within the next eight hours at least."

Eight hours later they sat over the fire in the drawing room. Anne Bradford had returned to the Manor in time for dinner and had told them all she knew about Beth's disappearance, the note which Evelyn Furnas had left at two o'clock in the morning, and Julia Seagreave's attempt to drive Beth away from the house by telling her she was the cause of Anne's not marrying Haswell.

The latter gave a sharp exclamation when he heard that. "Good Lord, Anne, I am responsible for that."

"How could you be, Jim?"

"Because after you had promised to marry me—is it possible that was only last night?—I met Chris and Beth in the lobby. I told Chris I'd asked you and I said, oh, I don't know what, but something about how hard it was to wait. What I meant, of course, was that any delay was hard, but on top of what Julia said to her, Beth could have misunderstood it."

"So that's explained," Anne said in relief. "Beth must have started out with Mark Craven of her own free will, thinking she was helping us. But she won't marry him; her good strong common sense will come to her rescue. Whatever Craven intends—"

"Where is she?" Chris cried. "Where is she?"

"The police will find her," Haswell said, trying to speak with more assurance than he felt.

"In time, yes. But meanwhile—"

Anne went to his side and touched his cheek gently with her fingers. "Chris," she said softly. "Chris."

His jaw rippled as he forced his teeth together. She turned away with the helpless suffering of the mother who cannot take upon herself her children's griefs, and went out of the room. She walked quickly up the stairs to the tutor's room and opened the door noiselessly.

Smith lay in bed, his face waxen, eyelids closed, his face oddly empty of expression, a white bandage around his head. Rose was on her knees beside the bed, both her hands clasping one of his, which she held against her cheek. Tears rolled down her face while she looked at him. After a moment, Anne stepped back and closed the door again.

Why was the maid so grief-stricken over the tutor's accident? Could she be responsible for it?

When she returned to the drawing room she shook her head in response to the mute question in the three faces that turned to hers. "No change," she said.

The hours passed. Now and then Chris paced the floor. Several times he had suggested that his mother go to bed but she refused.

"I couldn't sleep. It would be easier to wait here with you."

During the night a violent storm lashed at the trees and beat on the windows. Beth is somewhere out in that storm, Chris thought. Beth, Beth, my darling, where are you?

The storm died down at last and there was a faint rim of light on the eastern horizon. Chris got up stiffly and replenished the fire. His mother dozed uneasily in her chair. Colonel Haswell sat brooding in his. Ted got up and stretched.

"I'll make some coffee," he suggested. "No use waking the servants."

Chris went upstairs and opened the door to Smith's room. There seemed to be no change. Rose sat quietly beside the bed, wide awake, her eyes on his face. Chris was about to back out of the room when the tutor moved his head slightly and moaned. In a moment Rose had leaned forward and taken his hand in hers.

The waxen lids fluttered open. From his vantage point Chris could see that the eyes were blank at first; then, as a hand groped for the bandage, a look of pain flickered across the white face; then the eyes focused on Rose. A faint smile touched his mouth.

"Rose," he whispered.

"Don't try to talk, Mr. Smith," the girl said, her voice low.

"What's wrong? What happened to me? Why are you here?"

"I'll tell you if you promise to keep still." She went on quickly, her voice still low, with a new gentleness in it which Chris had never heard before. "I found you under the bushes at the edge of the woods. Someone had struck you on the head. We brought you in here and got you a doctor."

"Under the bushes!" the tutor exclaimed in surprise.

He had not, Chris observed, showed surprise at the idea that someone had struck him. It was being found under the bushes that had caused that exclamation.

"Shh!" the girl warned him.

"And you have been taking care of me?"

The girl nodded, the color beginning to come back to her face under the intentness of his gaze.

"You are—very sweet, Rose. You increase my debt to you."

"Please don't talk," she begged him.

"I won't awaken anyone," he promised her.

"It's for your sake, not for theirs. Anyhow, no one went to bed last night."

"Why not? Don't tell me," and there was a touch of bitterness in his voice, "that the Bradfords care whether I was killed or not."

"It's Miss Beth. She's been kidnaped."

"What!" This time the tutor sat bolt upright, his hands clutching his head as pain racked it.

"Lie still," Rose said.

"No, go out of the room. I'm going to get up."

Something in his tone made the girl get reluctantly to her feet. Chris ran swiftly down the stairs. In a few moments he saw the girl come out of Smith's room.

He went to the door of the drawing room. "Ted," he said quietly, "keep an eye on Smith's balcony, will you? He is conscious and he's getting up, but he's not going to get away."

"I don't believe he'll try it," Ted said stubbornly.

Ten minutes later the tutor's door opened and he came out, staggering. Rose, who had been waiting outside his door, ran to him.

"You shouldn't be doing this," she protested.

He smiled down at her. "My faithful little friend,"

he said tenderly. "My faithful little friend. I'll have to ask one more thing of you, Rose. Let me lean on you. My legs don't seem to be willing to hold me up." He put his arm around her shoulders and leaned heavily against her. One step at a time he went down the stairs, clinging to her, until he reached the drawing room door.

Chris was waiting for him. "Come in, Mr. Smith," he said.

Rose eased the wounded man into a chair and then stood beside him like a sentinel.

A gesture from Chris silenced his mother, who had been about to ask Smith how he felt.

"What happened to you?"

The tutor leaned his head against the back of the chair, his eyes staring myopically without his glasses.

"I was walking," he said, speaking slowly and with difficulty, "and someone struck me over the head. It was dark under the trees and I couldn't see who it was."

Chris shook his head. "You'll have to do better than that," he said, a new hard note in his voice. "You weren't walking and you weren't under the trees and it wasn't dark. You were struck over the head in my study and I think you were rifling my safe at the time. Well, Smith?"

The tutor lifted his head and saw Ted's expression. "Sorry," he said. "I won't talk until—"

And then, unbelievably, there was a revolver in Chris's hand. "You'd better talk and talk fast, Smith."

Something changed in the tutor's face. It was alert, intent, keenly awake to what was going on. In the distance there was a wailing of sirens which drew nearer, screaming, but no one noticed. They were all absorbed by the drama within the room itself.

"You can't kill me, Bradford," Smith said confidently. There was hatred in his voice but there was not a trace of fear. "You are too cowardly to kill before witnesses. And there are two witnesses here who believe in me, your brother Ted and Rose." His hand reached up and clasped hers. "No, you won't kill me before witnesses. You'd do it as you killed Gilbert, in the dark." No one could have mistaken the blazing conviction in the man's voice.

It was Colonel Haswell who recovered first from his profound shock and saw that the room was filled with people. Four people, actually: two uniformed policemen; his missing butler, Stone; and, unbelievably, Beth Gilbert.

And it was Stone, who at first glance appeared to be a prisoner, who took the situation into his own hands.

He stood for a moment summing it up and then he stepped forward. "Put down that gun, Bradford," he said. "The game is up. At last we're going to have the truth."

XVIII

At last we're going to have the truth. Beth had
dropped into a chair near the door, with the words
ringing in her ears. Chris still held that small, ugly-
looking revolver leveled at Smith, who lay back in a
chair, his face ghastly pale, a white bandage around
his head. He looked like a dying man, helpless, injured, and yet Chris watched him grimly, without
pity. Oh, Chris, Chris!

The two policemen stood back, not interfering, but
watchful, hands on their guns. During that long drive
home the policeman driving Stone's car had said little.

"Kidnaping," he had remarked once. "He'll be sorry
he was born."

"But it wasn't Mr. Stone who kidnaped me," Beth
had protested. He's a detective. He saved me. He was
taking me home."

"Yeah? Then why is there a general order out to
pick him up?"

Beth had been too confused to find an answer. Her
eyes felt tight from lack of sleep but she could not
sleep. As they drove, her mind leaped restlessly from
one thought to another and all of them were be-
wildering, frightening. Pictures crowded on one another: the note lying on her dresser in the hotel;
Julia telling her that she was spoiling Nan's life;
Craven dragging her into the little shack in the woods;
Stone's face, a shapeless white blob, pressed against
the dark windowpane. She shook with a nervous
tremor.

"It's all right," the policeman had said, his voice
big and comforting. "Nothing is going to hurt you
now."

"I—know," she had answered shakily.

The miracle of recurring morning had filled the sky. Light was followed by the colors of late fall, the rusty reds and soft browns and dull greens, like a faded Oriental rug. Here and there rows of pumpkins glowed brightly in stripped cornfields. The air was sparklingly bright, clean-washed by the rain.

At last they had arrived at familiar territory again, rolling down the village street, turning into the curving driveway that led to the Manor.

And then they had come upon that incredible tableau. Chris holding a gun on the helpless Smith, who was crying out that Chris—Chris!—had murdered her father. And he believed it.

And then Stone had stepped forward. "At last we're going to have the truth."

For a moment Chris looked at Beth and something leaped in his eyes. He half rose to go to her. Then he looked at Stone and his eyes traveled on to the policemen who waited in the background.

He spoke tranquilly. "Glad to see you, officer. So you picked him up! Arrest these two men."

"What's your charge?" one of the policemen asked.

"Murder," Chris said. "The murder of Charles Gilbert two years ago."

"Stone!" Smith exclaimed in horror.

The detective shook his head. "Let him put the rope around his own neck," he said coolly. "Then we'll do our talking."

Rapidly Chris outlined the story of Gilbert, the missing formula and the two men who had been associated with it: his assistant Larry Sergent, and his unidentified partner.

"For two years I've tried to smoke out the assistant and discover the identity of the partner. A month ago I announced that I had the formula and that I was going to exploit it. Within a matter of days things began to happen. The first was Smith's application for the job of Ted's tutor. That was my fault. His experience seemed to be just what I wanted and I didn't check on his references. I took him at his face value until Colonel Haswell's butler left and he wanted another.

"In a small community like this, of course, everyone knows about everyone else. So when I dropped into the telegraph office one day the clerk said, 'That's a nice guy you have tutoring Mr. Ted. I see he helped Colonel Haswell get a butler.' He showed me a copy of a telegram from Smith to Stone, *Haswell needs a butler. Find him one.*"

Chris paused for a moment and then went on. "At that point I began to be interested in John Smith. He and Stone have been meeting secretly. Smith has prowled endlessly around this house and gone through the desk in my study. They have held secret meetings on the place here. Smith got poison ivy by climbing down the pillars of his balcony so he wouldn't be seen going out the front door.

"Lately our new maid Rose, who also appeared at the time I made my announcement, has been eavesdropping whenever she got a chance. For her benefit, Colonel Haswell and I staged a conversation in which I said that the formula was in the safe; I left the combination where she could find it. What happened? Smith tried to open this safe last night."

"Who is this man?" one of the policemen asked.

"I don't know his real name," Chris admitted. "I think he is Gilbert's unidentified partner."

It was Stone who answered him. "You are wrong," he said. "Smith wasn't Gilbert's partner, he was his assistant, Larry Sergent." He turned to the two officers. "Suppose you let me do some talking, or is Bradford so important in this community that—"

"Hold it," the policeman said coldly. "Every man gets a fair break in this community. We don't play favorites."

Smith—Sergent?—laughed bitterly. "A fair break!" he said.

Beth looked on in dazed incredulity. Was she asleep? Was this some feverish dream? She glanced furtively around the room. No, she could hear the clock tick, hear the sizzle of the fire, see Nan and

Ted, white with shock; Colonel Jim leaning forward intently; Chris, cool and suddenly hard, suddenly remote; Smith, frighteningly pale but with an eagerness about him, almost a look of hope. She put out her hand gropingly and Ted came over and curled up at her feet, more as though he were seeking comfort than offering it. Her hand touched his arm. She was awake, horribly awake. With a need for something real, something human to cling to, she rested her arm on Ted's shoulder and leaned lightly against him as she studied the two men, Chris and Smith, who faced one another in the still room.

"Yes," Smith said, his voice weak but steady, "I am Larry Sergent. I was Charles Gilbert's chemical assistant for ten years, during which we devoted all our time, day and night, to developing his formula for plastics. He was completely wrapped up in the laboratory and so was I. He had taken me out of school and given me my first job because he was impressed by some experiments I had done on my own. He was a— a fine man to work for.

"Well, you know that after a number of disappointments he finally achieved what he had set out to do. But during the last three years of his life he changed quite a lot in personality. He sacrificed everything for the sake of his work; he had long before given up his daughter, his home life, even any social life. Little by little, he became secretive. As he realized what a tremendous thing he had, he began to distrust people. I believe, in a way, I was the only person he completely trusted."

Chris laughed scornfully and Sergent's face flushed.

"I can prove that," he said quietly. "I *will* prove it. But he didn't trust anyone altogether. I knew that he was in touch with someone who was interested in becoming his partner and putting up the funds necessary for manufacturing the formula. But he would not tell me who it was. This much I do know—he did not trust the partner. Because the night he left to meet him and settle the partnership papers, he took with him a substitute formula."

"What became of the real one?" Chris demanded, leaning forward.

"He gave it to me," Sergent said.

"*Gave* it to you!" Chris exclaimed.

"Entrusted it to me," Sergent corrected. "That night he went to the Manor—and he never left there. When he was found, he had been robbed and the substitute formula was gone—much good did it do the man who stole it!"

There was a pause while he tried to gather his thoughts together. Rose went to a table and brought him a glass of water. He thanked her with a faint smile, sipped it and then went on.

"Someone was very busy that night. Apparently the thief was bitterly disappointed after killing Gilbert to discover that his terrible risk had been taken for nothing. He came after me. I was working late in the laboratory, straightening up and clearing up records because Mr. Gilbert had said we would take off a month for a holiday. I was bending over the desk when something soft was drawn tight over my nose and eyes. The cloth was soaked in chloroform and I lost consciousness. After that I didn't know anything more until I came to on a freight train. When I managed to get off at a siding I made my way to the nearest town, intending to call the police. Then I saw the newspapers, with the account of Gilbert's death and robbery."

There was a long silence this time, as though he was gathering his strength.

"Well," he said at last, "I didn't call the police."

"Why not?" Chris snapped.

Again there was bitterness in Sergent's laugh. "Because," he said, "I had the real formula. Don't you see? And I had no proof that I had not killed Gilbert and robbed him to get it. There wasn't a scrap of evidence that he had taken a substitute with him. By that time, the hue and cry was out for me and I knew perfectly well that I didn't have a chance." He challenged Chris. "Would you have believed me if I had come to you with a story like that?"

"No."

"And yet," Sergent said, "you are the only one who could have believed me. Because *you killed Gilbert.* It took me a long time to figure that out. It wasn't until the missing partner failed to put in an appearance that it dawned on me there was no other man. That you had been the partner all along. I knew then that if I was ever to have proof that would clear me, I'd have to come here. Proof of that partnership between you and Gilbert must exist somewhere.

"I finally got in touch with Stone, who is not only a private detective but a distant cousin of mine, and he believed me. His loyalty and faith in me just about saved my reason. I didn't tell him the whole truth. I didn't dare admit, even to him, that I had the formula. At his own expense he followed Miss Gilbert through Europe, sure that somewhere she must have it. I wanted to come here to the Manor, so when I saw Bradford's advertisement for a tutor I jumped at it. When he announced that he was going to manufacture the formula I told Stone the truth. He returned from Europe and, when Haswell needed a butler, he applied for the job."

"I'll say one thing: you've been a swell tutor," Ted put in, speaking for the first time.

Chris had put the revolver down on the desk. He was watching Sergent intently. There was a change in his voice. "Sergent," he said, "you are lying. Oh, I believe you are Sergent. I even believe you have the formula. I believe you were chloroformed and kidnaped. But—you are holding something back. What is it?"

Sergent did not reply.

"How did you get the combination to my safe?"

Sergent shook his head.

"I gave it to him," Rose confessed. "He is trying to protect me. I gave it to him."

"Who knocked you out, Sergent?" Chris demanded. He leaned forward impatiently. "What are you afraid of, man?" Still Sergent did not speak, torn by uncertainty. "You can speak now," Chris begged him.

"You see, since you began to talk, *I have seen the truth.*"

The eyes of the two men met and locked. No one breathed. The two policemen waited, rigid.

Sergent hesitated so long that Beth's nerves screamed.

Chris spoke again. "I know the truth. But I cannot prove it. Can you? Together we—"

Sergent's hands twisted together. "How do I know that I can trust you?"

Chris grinned boyishly. "You'll have to take a chance on me," he said.

Rose intervened, "Mr. Smith—Mr. Sergent," she said. "You can trust Mr. Chris."

"How about you?"

"It doesn't matter about me," the maid assured him. "Truly it doesn't."

Abruptly the tutor made up his mind. "All right," he agreed. "All that I had in the way of proof of identity as to the missing partner was an unsigned note from him which Gilbert had left behind. Handwritten. As I told you, the more I thought about it, the more I came to the conclusion that you were the man. Then I came here as Ted's tutor and I hunted until I found a specimen of your handwriting. And I knew then I was on the wrong track."

"Then why," Ted demanded, "did you accuse Chris just now of being the murderer?"

The tutor turned around and met the boy's eyes squarely. "Because I am a hunted man, living under a false name. All the weight of the evidence is against me; I have no way of clearing myself, no money, nothing but the friendship and faith of Stone." He smiled at Rose. "And Rose," he added. "But Mr. Bradford has money and position. He can fight where I can't. By leaving it up to him, I had a chance that the truth would come out."

"Go back to your unsigned letter," Chris said. "Is that all the proof you have?"

"No. Thanks to Rose," Sergent said, "I have identified the man who wrote that letter. Are you sure—?"

he looked questioningly at the maid. She nodded her head.

"Well, I couldn't live in this house without noticing that Rose was trying to find out things about the family. Any clue was worth following so I watched her. Somehow I could not believe she was a common criminal; she struck me as being a victim. I began following her." He described the evening when he had trailed her to the movie and their conversation afterwards.

"As you know, Rose had the combination to the safe, and she gave it to me so that I could prevent the other man from stealing the formula. But before she handed me the combination she gave me, by mistake, another note. And the handwriting was the same as that of Gilbert's missing partner. There could be no mistake. I had studied that writing so long I knew every quirk of it. And the man who had written it was Mark Craven."

Rose nodded. "He sent me here to look for the formula. You can arrest me now. I—I'm glad it's over."

Anne Bradford stirred in her chair as though aroused from a terrible dream. "But why, Rose? Why did you consent to do that?"

"Because I had to," Rose said. "Because—"

There was the deep throbbing roar of a powerful motor outside and a car door slammed. The front door opened and someone came rapidly down the hall to the drawing room.

Craven stood in the doorway. He did not see the two policemen against the wall. His usually colorless eyes were aflame, his face crimson and dark with anger as he approached Beth Gilbert. With a little cry she shrank closer to Ted, who scrambled to his feet.

"Well," Craven said softly, "you've given me quite a chase. I've driven like mad to make up for the time this fellow made me lose by tinkering with my motor."

"Don't touch her," Chris snapped, as Craven's hand reached for Beth's arm.

Craven smiled. "Touch her? It's not the first time.

Your ward and I were together for hours and hours last night, Bradford. So I think there will be no difficulty about our marriage. Come on, Beth." His lips twitched. "You can't afford any scandal, you know."

Chris was leaping for him, the two policemen were stepping forward to intervene, when Martha Mumford came breathlessly into the room. Little, wrinkled, old, but with the mien of an avenging nemesis.

"For the land's sake, Mark Craven," she demanded, "how many wives do you want?"

XIX

There was a tiny fleck of foam on Craven's lips. He swore below his breath.

"Mummy," Chris said, "I think you had better leave us now. I'll see you later."

"You'd better listen to me now, Chris. What I've got to say has a lot to do with what's going on here." The old eyes swept the room shrewdly. "But it's a long story and I guess, if you don't mind, I'll sit down."

She swayed on her feet and Stone hastily pushed forward a chair and guided her into it. After a moment or two she looked up with her queer, crackly laugh.

"I've been traveling, Chris, and I'm not used to it."

"Mummy!"

There was a very passion of impatience in that one word.

"I know, Chris. I know how you feel. I'll be just as quick as I can. Rose came to see me the other night and she told me a long story. Mostly about Mr. Mark Craven here. He's been threatening, if she didn't do what he wanted, to tell something the poor girl's ashamed of. Rose didn't know what to do at first, then she made up her mind that she didn't care what became of her and she told me the whole story. All about her life—the mistakes she made and then—oh, you scoundrel!"—Martha Mumford shook her fist at Craven—"then she said she had married that man and after a month he told her that the marriage was a fake."

"That's not true," Craven snapped. "I never married this girl. A housemaid? The whole thing is preposterous, made up by a meddling, troublemaking old fool of a woman."

191

"That will do, Craven," Chris said, his voice hard. "Women are not insulted in this house." As Craven muttered, he added, "Let her finish her story." His voice was grim.

Craven looked around, as though in search of someone who would believe him. For the first time he saw the two policemen standing quietly against the wall. His face turned gray.

"Well," Martha Mumford went on, "I got to thinking. There was a movie I saw not too long ago that had the same plot. The man married the girl, then preferred a richer one but didn't want any news of the first marriage to get out, as it was bound to do if he arranged a divorce. But he took a chance on the girl not saying anything and claimed the marriage was a fake.

"Rose is kind of silly in some ways but she is not a fool. She would have known if that marriage was not on the up and up. Marriage means a lot to a girl. She didn't have the license—Craven had taken that away from her—but she remembered the place and the name of the justice of the peace who married them.

"So I decided it was the same thing as the movie. Only I didn't know how to go at proving it. First I tried to call you but the phone didn't answer."

Beth raised her head with a guilty start but no one noticed; all eyes were fixed on Martha.

"There's no truer saying, Chris, than that one about casting your bread upon the waters. I looked up a boy that I'd helped through law school and told him what I was after. And he paid back all I had ever done for him in the help he gave me. He was quite excited. He checked up on the little town in Maryland where Rose says she was married and, sure enough, he found the records. I'm mighty glad for Rose in one way but terribly sorry for her to be tied to a creature like that."

"Then," Beth said, her lips white, "if you were already married, what did you intend to do with me?"

Craven did not meet her eyes. Bradford, with a

growl of rage, sprang at Craven, but Stone was too quick for him.

"Hold it, Mr. Bradford," he said quietly. "The law's here. He's their baby." Still holding Chris's arm, he turned to indicate Craven. "You've been hunting a thief who attempted to steal the Gilbert formula. Well, there's your man. He thought he would outsmart Gilbert and get the formula without having to share the profits. But Gilbert somehow distrusted him. That's why he took a substitute with him."

"I remember," Chris said, "Craven asking me if I was sure I had the 'right' formula.

"He killed Charles Gilbert to get it; he used a girl's fear and shame to help him find the right one; he attempted to force Miss Gilbert into marriage in order to have legal control over it; he—"

"He knocked me out yesterday," Smith—or rather, Sergent—said in his faint voice, "when I tried to look through the safe to find what Bradford had in the way of records. I knew it could not be the real formula."

Craven's face was ghastly, his eyes were hideous in their malignity.

"That's a damned lie! You can't prove any of this."

Stone pulled out of his billfold the unsigned memorandum which Sergent had found about Gilbert's records and laid it beside the note which Rose had given Sergent.

Craven laughed. "What do they prove? That I was to be Gilbert's partner? I acknowledge that. But not—"

There was a ring of triumph in Stone's voice. "That's not all!" he exclaimed. "While you were here knocking out Smith yesterday so that you could go through Bradford's safe before you drove to New York, I was at the inn going through your papers. Among them I found Gilbert's wallet and the letters he had in his pocket *at the time he was killed.* How do you explain that, Mark Craven?"

One of the policemen moved away from the wall. "All right, Stone, I guess that's enough. There's a court case there, all right. We'll take care of him now."

He slipped handcuffs on the cringing man who stood at bay. "What about this kidnaping charge?"

"Not kidnaping," Stone said. "We want him for murder."

The drawing room at the Manor was rosy with firelight and the glow from shaded lamps. Outside, the first snow of the season swirled softly against the windows. Anne Bradford came down the stairs in a gown which shimmered and gleamed like frost in moonlight. Martha Mumford followed in a voluminous gray dress, with an apron which almost extinguished the skirt. She carried an evening wrap of violet velvet which had a deep collar of ermine.

"Are you sure this will be warm enough, Miss Anne?" the older woman queried anxiously. "When a storm sets in early in December like this it sometimes turns into a blizzard."

"What a baby you try to make of me, Mummy, and you still call me Miss Anne as you did when I was a young girl. What a relative thing age is! To you I am young, to Ted and Beth—well, if not old, I seem to be perilously near the verge of old age; to myself—why, Mummy, I feel as though I had just begun to know what real living is. I am conscious of deeper purposes, illimitable opportunities; I have acquired a philosophy which helps me to see things in their right proportions, the big things big and the small things small. What does youth know of the magnificent emotions and possibilities of middle age?"

Martha Mumford shook her head sagely. "Middle age doesn't mean the same to everyone, Miss Anne. It is a time of life when all the forces in a body are at their height, and if a person has lived an unrestrained, selfish youth, the very strength of personality will sweep him on in a current of self-indulgence. If he hasn't struggled to get the better of disagreeable traits of character these will become dominant, and without the charm of youth to soften them they will prove unbearable to his friends.

"Middle age is a time of realization, all right, but it depends upon what one has done with the preceding years. You've done the very best you could always; you've kept a firm hand on the wheel of your life and the compass steadily pointing toward the best. Your children, the neighbors, the finest man in this town adore you; why shouldn't you find life a wonderful, inspiring thing? That's what the good Lord meant it to be for us all."

"Mummy, you're a philosopher and a—a dear," Anne Bradford cried with an unsteady laugh. "Don't worry about my being warm. The car is heated and I have not far to go. Have you seen Beth?"

"She spoke to me as I passed her room. Said she would be down in a moment. She doesn't seem like her bright, happy self to me, Miss Anne. She hasn't tried to tease me once since I came."

Anne Bradford gazed thoughtfully into the fire. "I have noticed it. Something happened when we were in New York for the Towle debut. That day she was radiantly happy, bubbling over with youth and joy. She was asleep when I went out the next morning and when I returned she had gone with—she had gone with Mark Craven. I shall never forget the agony of that afternoon. Then came the revelations that our Mr. Smith was Larry Sergent, the missing assistant; that Colonel Haswell's butler was a private detective; and the duplicity and crime of Mark Craven."

"When is Chris coming back from New York?"

"He has said nothing in his letters about returning. He has been gone so long and I wish he could come. He would find out what is troubling Beth. It is the Gilbert formula which is keeping him, and working with the police in preparation for the Craven murder trial. How is Rose tonight?"

"Better, much better. She was lucky to get out of all her misery and unhappiness without a nervous breakdown. Land's sakes, what hasn't that girl been through! And all because she wanted money and the things money can buy. There are lots of girls like her, though."

"Yes, but can you wonder? They are young; they have a conviction that in the scheme of things it was intended that they should be beautiful, have lovely clothes and admiration lavished upon them. Poor children."

"Miss Anne, it beats me how you understand. You who have always had all you want. Most people would think the girls were weak fools."

"Do you think I have never been tempted, Mummy? I can forgive and pity Rose but I can't understand Mark Craven. He had made a fortune and yet he would steal—he would kill—to get more."

"Miss Anne, a man with the ambition to have more and more money is bound to be ruthless. It is a poisonous germ in his blood and the scientists haven't yet found a way to cure it."

"Do you think he—"

Martha nodded soberly. "There is no doubt about it. He will be found guilty. It's an ugly business and a tragic one for Rose to go through. But eventually she will have her freedom. The only reason she agreed to help him here was sheer terror lest he tell you about the bucket shop business and that you would set her adrift. She about worships you, Miss Anne."

"What will become of her?"

Martha smiled wisely. "I guess Mr. Sergent will take care of that. Poor things, with their heavy loads to bear, they turned naturally to each other for comfort. And now that Chris is giving him that fine position, working on the plastics, he will be able to support a wife." She broke off to say, "Here's Beth now."

Anne Bradford looked up keenly for a moment as the girl came into the room, then became engrossed in a detail of her cape to hide the mist which clouded her eyes at the sight of the change in the girl she loved so dearly. Beth wore a long white wool dinner dress, her hair was burnished from brushing, her face pale, her eyes shadowed.

"You won't be lonely, will you, Beth?" she asked cheerfully. "I wouldn't go if the dinner weren't being given for Colonel Jim and me. You'll have to dine alone. You know Ted—"

"Do I know Ted! My dear Nan, he has been arraying himself for the last three hours to do honor to the little Blossom's first dinner party. He's in a fever. His hair is plastered to his head and shines like a seal coat. Last time I saw him he was laboring to smooth down one refractory lock on the crown of his head." Her laugh was genuine.

Anne Bradford drew a quick sigh of relief. Surely the girl could have nothing very serious on her mind if she could laugh like that.

"I told Kate to serve your dinner here before the fire. It will be cozy and I don't have to think of you all alone in that big dining room."

Ted Bradford came tumultuously down the stairs, immaculately appareled in evening clothes, the ends of a white tie dangling down over his shirt front.

"Tie it for me, will you, Beth? I mussed up a bunch of them upsairs. I can't get the darned things even."

The girl strangled back a laugh as she looked at his distressed face.

"Cheer up, Theodore. The party won't begin without you. And how you'll set the little Blossom's heart to palpitating."

"Quit your kidding and help a fellow."

He peered into the mirror, smoothed his hair.

"Come away from that glass and sit on the arm of the chair, you giant, while I fix your tie. There, that is perfect. Now you may gaze at yourself in admiration."

He hurried to the mirror. His brows met in a critical frown. "The ends are not quite even." He seized the tie and began to twitch it.

"Let that alone," wailed Beth as she pulled away his hands. "Nan, take the boy away. Theodore," she added with exaggerated concern, "do let me lay your muffler about your shoulders."

"Hey, I told you you'd jam that tie." He rushed to the mirror and patted it anxiously.

Then he turned and with courtly deference offered his arm to his mother. When they had gone, Martha Mumford finished arranging a small round table in front of the fire. She laid her hand gently on the girl's shoulder. "Something is troubling you, Beth. When Chris comes home, tell him about it. He will make it all right."

"Tell Chris!" Beth stared wistfully into the fire. She had not seen him since that day when the policemen had brought her back from the mad trip with Craven.

After dinner she tried to read, played softly on the piano for a while, then seated herself at the desk and wrote furiously for about ten minutes. At the end of that time she began to nibble her pen and gaze fixedly into the fire, to pace slowly from the fire to the window. The snow still fell with feathery daintiness. There were partly obliterated wheel tracks on the drive. Who had come tonight? She turned quickly to see Christopher Bradford standing in the doorway, regarding her intently. He was in dinner clothes.

"Chris," she whispered, "is it really you?"

He laughed boyishly at her surprise.

"It really is. Don't stare as though I were a ghost, Beth. I arrived half an hour ago, had a bite brought to my room while I dressed, and here I am. Aren't you going to say that you are glad to see me?"

He advanced with outstretched hands. Something happened to her breath as she met his look.

"Of course I am, Chris." She turned away in an attempt to escape the compelling power of Bradford's eyes. His hands tightened on hers.

"You have something to tell me, Beth," he said in a quietly determined tone. "Let's get it over and have it behind us."

He still held her hands as he seated himself and tried to draw her down beside him. She sank to the ottoman beside his chair.

"I'd rather be here, please. What do you want to know, Chris?" Her long lashes hid her eyes and she bit her lips to keep them from trembling.

He held up her hand. "First, where is our wonder-ful-day ring?"

A wave of color stained her face. "Upstairs. I haven't worn it since—there was something—"

He put his hand under her chin and lifted her face. "What has happened, Beth?" he asked with a cool, matter-of-fact friendliness which instantly brought her eyes to his. "There, that's better. I can't talk to the top of your head. Now tell me what happened, dear."

He released her hands and she clasped them on his knee.

Hesitatingly at first, she told him the whole story, from the moment of her return when she had heard Evelyn Furnas break her engagement because of her, to Evelyn's threat to win Chris back, saying he was interested only in the formula, to Julia's accusation that she was standing in the way of Nan's happiness. She kept her eyes on his even when she saw a little white line settle about his lips.

"So then, when Mark—" she steadied her voice— "when he asked me to marry him, I thought it would be best for—everyone." She added pathetically, "Are you very angry with me?"

"Angry, my darling? Only dumb with horror at what might have happened to you."

She clung to his hands. "But it didn't happen. It couldn't have happened. Something would have saved me at the last moment. When he kissed me—" The little shiver she gave brought his eyes smoldering with fury to hers.

"Anyhow," she said, with more determination, "we've got to make sure that Nan and the colonel marry without any more delay."

Chris laughed. "Where have you been?" he teased her. "Don't you know they are going to be married at Christmas?" He stood up, looking down at her.

"No. I—I'm glad."

"Beth." He drew her to her feet, into his arms. "I love you very much. Do you think—do I seem too old?—I'd take such good care of you; you'd be safe with me, my darling, my lovely darling."

"Chris—"

His arms tightened. His eyes glowed down into hers. He pressed his lips to hers in passionate tenderness. He kissed her again and again, then laughed exultantly as two soft arms stole around his neck.

"Do you love me, Beth?"

"Oh, Chris, so terribly much! It happened all of a sudden, one night when I was walking into this room for dinner and all at once—there was only—you, deep in my heart, filling it to the very brim."

The outside door slammed. "Hey, Beth!" The words trailed off as Ted Bradford stood transfixed in the doorway. Then he turned, bounded up the stairs, singing at the top of his young voice:

> *Here comes the bride!*
> *Here comes the bride!*